TEARDROPS AT SUNSET

RICHARD AKOJI

First published 1984 by Macmillan Publishers

Second edition published 2025- Cover design, artwork, illustration, edited text, collaboration, revised, arranged

© NEO BOOKS 2025

This edition Reprinted in 2025 by NEO BOOKS with AUTHORIZATION & PERMISSION FROM AUTHOR

NEOANCESTORIES@GMAIL.COM

ISBN: 979-8-89693-099-0

Contents

Pacesetters series

All the novels in the Pacesetters series deal with contemporary issues and problems in a way that is particularly designed to interest young adults, although the stories are such that they will appeal to all ages.

Titles in the series Pacesetters series

- *Director!* by Agbo Areo
- *The Smugglers* by Kalu Okpi
- *The Undesirable Element* by Mohammed Sule
- *Christmas in the City* by Afari Assan
- *Felicia* by Rosina Umelo
- *The Betrayer* by Sam Adewoye
- *The Hopeful Lovers* by Agbo Areo
- *The Delinquent* by Mohammed Sule
- *The Worshippers* by Victor Thorpe
- *On the Road* by Kalu Okpi
- *Too Cold for Comfort* by Jide Oguntoye

- *For Mbatha and Rabeka* by David Maillu
- *The Instrument* by Victor Thorpe
- *The Wages of Sin* by Ibe Oparandu
- *Bloodbath at Lobster Close* by Dickson Ighavini
- *Evbu My Love* by Helen Ovbiagele
- *Mark of the Cobra* by Valentine Alily
- *The Black Temple* by Mohmed Tukur Garba
- *Stone of Vengeance* by Victor Thorpe
- *Sisi* by Yemi Sikuade
- *Death is a Woman* by Dickson Ighavini
- *Tell Me No More* by Senzenjani Lukhele
- *State Secret* by Hope Dube
- *Love on the Rocks* by Andrew Sesinyi
- *The Equatorial Assignment* by David Maillu
- *Have Mercy* by Joseph Mangut
- *The Cyclist* by Philip Phil-Ebosie
- *Agony in Her Voice* by Peter Katuliiba
- *Naira Power* by Buchi Emecheta
- *Cross-Fire!* by Kalu Okpi

This book is dedicated to my sister

Rose Akoji

Chapter 1

A whimpering noise is coming from the folding cot in a corner of the inner room, disturbing the dream-like atmosphere of the house. The crying is coming from my baby, my daughter. I gave birth to her less than four months ago, unwillingly. She is an illegitimate child, if you understand that word 'illegitimate' to mean 'illegal', 'contrary to the law', at least the law that should govern the birth of children in a similar situation. A friend has just called on me with an envelope bearing a foreign stamp. It is addressed to me and postmarked London. The letter inside has flown all the way from a long-forgotten friend. Oh, no, no!! That word 'forgotten' is not fitting.

Since he left the country, I have not lived through a single day without thinking about him. He meant a great deal to me and this morning I've decided to put everything down on paper, to try and explain what made him leave the country on that chilly morning. I am home sick this morning because of a debilitating headache, the kind that keeps on opening your skull when you feel dejected or depressed. I need time to be by myself so I have asked Dr. Okon, the father of that 'illegal' baby who is squalling away now, to give me a 'doctor's sick report' that will give me some days of rest away from the office. He did not make any objections and has given me a certificate for three days off. I took it to the personnel manager of the Leventis Stores in Kano, where I work. He is a very kind man, and has always been ready to help me. Without any questions he has agreed to my having the time off. I know I have disappointed him greatly. I am guilty and I know that many people, when they hear all about what happened to a young girl like myself, will place the blame on me and say, 'Look, girl, you deserve what has happened to you.' But others will surely sympathize with me.

My hands tremble as I read through the short letter. In spite of its brevity, it seems endless. Several hours later, I am still lingering over a single line, or staring at a phrase in another paragraph.

Hey Onyemowo,

I will be flying back home in a few weeks' time. The girl I plan to marry is here beside my bed in the hospital and is saying hello to you. We shall have the formal wedding in the church in my village when we are back in Nigeria. Well, Onyemowo, I have never yet seen a white girl and a black man getting married in our church, but we have decided that is what we want. Anyone going abroad hopes to bring home the new knowledge, but a man coming back home with a white wife can raise suspicions that he has not got himself a good housewife. The reason is that, more often than not, you get the white wife running away with her children, going back to her own country after several years of successful marriage. I'm not going to make the same mistake. I intend to marry in my own country and according to our laws. My girl agrees wholeheartedly with me. I want to ask you something special. Will you be our flower girl that day? I know you will agree because you will be glad that I've found the right girl as a wife. You won't disappoint me.

How are you getting on with Dr. Okon? Abubakar wrote recently to tell me you had got married to him. I felt very sad when I first heard the news. But after a while, I realized that it was not your fault. I knew you could not wait for me forever, not when you thought my condition was hopeless. Perhaps you should have waited to see me back home from the hospital abroad before taking the final decision to leave me. Hadn't you heard the news that your helpless boy was going to come back home a healthy man? It is fortunate indeed that I have found a nice girl with whom I can share the bitterness and joy that is life in Nigeria.

All the doctors here have been very kind to me. I have had the very best possible treatment. The white nurses have been marvelous too. Oh, I've just realized that I haven't yet told you that my girl is a staff nurse in this hospital. I can hardly believe that soon she will be my wife. Expect us any time now— we intend to leave on the 20th of this month.

Bye!! Idu Idoko

He is coming back with a white lady! Was it really my fault for leaving him for a while, hoping to go back to him later? Was I not doing him a good turn when I decided to turn to Dr. Okon? Has it been a mistake to submit to a man I hate for the sake of one I love dearly? I knew that Idu would never have recovered from that terrible accident if I had said 'No' to the demands of Dr. Okon. He would not have been flown out of the country to the specialist hospital abroad. I held out for the sake of fidelity to him. Surely he should have realized that I loved him dearly and had never at any time loved Dr. Okon? Despair and disappointment threaten to tear me apart.

With my red biro pen, I cross out the sentence in the letter that asks me to be their flower girl. Why should I play the part of the flower girl and not the part of a wife? No! The white girl must not show her face in the land of my forefathers. I will tell her that this is my country and the people living in it are my people. I will prove to her that I am the daughter of my country's soil and have no intention of letting her pollute it. I must be prepared for her coming, prepared to stop her driving through the gates of the airport. I must use all means and devices to stop her coming.

I didn't really understand what effect this would have as I dropped the letter, out of rage, onto the floor and went to the inner room to dress properly. I decide to go right away and tell that 'long throat' Abubakar that he is wrong about everything. But I changed my mind, abruptly. After all, he is right about the bare facts and I have already given my first baby to that man, my worst enemy. My daughter is still crying. Naomi, the little girl we have just employed to take care of my baby for me, has been sent on an errand and has not yet come back home to take care of her. Furious, I storm out of the bedroom and go back to the parlor to pick up the letter I dropped on the blue carpet. With the letter in my hand, I return to the little girl in the cot, bend down and hold the printed lines right in front of her tear-soaked eyes. 'Now read it!' I roar at the little child. But all the answer she can give me is a renewed outburst of frightened sobbing.

"Read it!' I barked again. She stops crying for an instant as if shocked into silence. 'Yes, you are now deciding to remain silent. Very soon this silence will turn to an everlasting silence and then you will cry no more... cry no more, I say!' Right inside the room there, beside the baby girl, I think over the various ways of getting rid of my daughter, but none of the ideas proves satisfactory. After all thoughts and ideas desert me, like a mad bitch, I seize her, shake her and then tightly press my hands over the tiny insect-like hole that is her mouth. I press her nostrils tightly, using my left palm. The letter drops from my hand unnoticed. I am determined to choke her to death. Before I can carry out my plan, I sense the approaching odor of a man's armpit. With blazing eyes, I look back and see Dr. Okon coming towards me. I leave the baby in fear and fall back heavily. The yellow-painted wall feels the weight of my head and I feel a sharp pain in my skull. 'Are you frightened by my unexpected appearance?' he asks, trying to gather me with him. In his voice I can feel a sense of tension. All I can stammer is 'Yes... yes.'

'There's no need to be so jumpy, unless of course...' he continues and he strides down to where the baby lies, her little chest heaving, panting. Seeing him moving forward to the cot, I jumped up in fright. This makes him wonder again what is really the matter with me. I know he suspects something. He looks at me in astonishment. I know for certain that my daughter will now regard me as her number one enemy, if indeed she has any enemies besides me. She cannot tell her troubles to her father and so I am able to escape the accusation that I have tried to murder my own daughter in cold blood—what a sensational piece of news that would have been when it was announced on the radio!

I try to pretend that I am not living with any man and that I have not given birth to any child. If it were only true! I don't want to be a mother. I only want … He looks at the baby, then glances at me and inclines his head. 'Why were you frightened by my coming?' he asks. He is a psychologist and I know he can read minds easily, or so he once told me—and I believed him. As he stands gazing at me, I know he is reading my mind; it seems like a dirty trick. I feel murderous. 'You know I have not been feeling well this... morning,' I stammered. 'Yes, yes, I know that very well. That's why I asked your boss to give you some days of rest.' I can hear an almost infantile anger bumping its head in his voice.

'What... what I really mean is that the baby is not feeling very good this morning and... and I have been feeling so nervous about her.' 'Go now and collect my stethoscope and the thermometer from the drawer. I will examine her thoroughly!' he orders. I go down to collect the instruments. But is the baby really sick? It stands to reason that her temperature will surely have risen some degrees above normal after my attempt to take her precious life. Why did I try to kill my daughter in cold blood? I will explain the reasons for this action later on. 'Here they are,' I say, handing the instruments to him. After a long and a close examination, Dr. Okon turns around. 'Both her temperature and breathing rate are a bit high... I will see what I can do about it. It is nothing serious, nothing to worry about. Everything will soon be normal.'

In my imagination, I fall to kiss the floor. I already know pretty well that everything will soon become normal. But she has only escaped for the moment. Next time she will pass away quickly without a warning bell, without the knowledge of her father, Dr. Okon. 'What are all these bruises on her face?' He is looking closely at the face of the baby. 'It is... nothing... It is...' I cannot say anything convincing.

'There's blood on the face of this innocent baby and yet you maintain it is nothing? Tell me what has really happened to my baby, onyemowo. Tell me...' He comes closer to me, takes my chin gently in his hand and looks me straight in the eyes. My lips cannot move to defend myself. He lets my jaw fall abruptly and shouts that I have done something to the baby and that I must tell him everything before he takes any action against me. He moves to where the baby lies, threatening to break my neck for me if I have touched her. His voice is now rising so high that I imagine it flying up like an evil bird to settle on the edge of the ceiling. 'She fell out of her cot,' I lied. 'But she cannot possibly fall out of this well-built cot. If she does fall out of it, then it means that we are at fault for not putting it up properly. Do you agree?'

He makes his way towards me and pushes me away from the side of the bed. Then he walks quickly to the door. Using the only key we have, he locks the door before returning to me and the baby. As I see him coming back, I know without being told that hot trouble is boiling up for me. I go to the little girl and pick her up in my arms, hoping to stop him from taking the wicked action he has in mind for me this afternoon. My enemy will be my savior at my time of trouble, I think as I hold the baby in my arms. But this cannot stop him from doing his work. He hurls himself at me and tears the baby from my arms. Then the thick belt begins to land on my flesh...

Chapter 2

As I washed my bruised and bloodied face the next morning, I realized how painful my nose was. My face really was a terrible sight. It looked as if a swarm of vicious wasps had stung me. Luckily, I still had one day's leave left. I even felt shy about appearing in front of Naomi and my daughter. For the sake of that baby I had been beaten up by Dr. Okon.

I felt like a stranger in Dr. Okon's house, like a fly caught in a spider's web. I could not escape him to return to my people for I knew perfectly well that they would not welcome me back. Apart from the opposition I could expect from my parents, the sight of the village itself would have automatically raised the most resistant hair on my head. I was no longer a part of the village. I belonged to the town into which I had married. To snatch me from its busy roads, its beauties, and its people of different colors and social behaviors, would be unthinkable. In the town, however, nobody knew me in terms of love. Nobody cared what I loved or hated. I could not go back to those who loved me, and I could not enjoy my freedom in the town. So, I was held at the crossroads. I went to the kitchen to warm up water to bathe my wounds again. I was desperate to repair or hide the damage as much as possible. I just could not stand any annoying questions from my co-workers. It was a terrible sight. I got the warm water from the fire, walked back and sat on the concrete floor of the kitchen. I dabbed my swollen face with a blue handkerchief. I took no notice of the throbbing pain I was now experiencing as a result of the hot water. I could stand anything that improved my appearance by the next morning. As I worked, I held my lips tightly between my teeth. Once or twice Naomi came over to me and asked what was the matter with my eyes and face. I told her that it was nothing to worry about and that my swollen face was from the previous night. She left me alone but I had the feeling that she was not satisfied with the reasons I had given her. Later, she came back again to ask, "Madam, wetin happen to...?" and she pointed her tiny fingers at my face.

"Your madam no sleep well well for night and na him do wey in eye come swell up this morning," I told her. Naomi was about ten years old. I did not know why she had been brought to this house to raise my baby for me and I had not found time to ask Dr. Okon about her. Maybe this was because I had no real interest in whether she stayed or went. One afternoon I suddenly saw her coming home with the father of my baby. Dr. Okon told me later that day that the girl was going to help me look after the baby. But why should this pretty young girl be prevented from finishing her education? I had wondered. Here she would not be able to attend a school. I had thought of bringing this to the notice of Dr. Okon, but thought it better to leave well alone because I needed someone to help me in the house. I had just come from the hospital with the newborn baby.

Naomi was a cheerful girl. She always had a smile even when things were difficult. I found joy in having her with me when I was sad with the world and with myself. She was a quick worker too—when she walked, I sometimes wondered if she had wings on her feet as she flew along. I knew very well that she would see through my lies about my face. Lying in an awkward position in bed overnight couldn't possibly have disfigured my face. Why did I have to lie to her? I asked myself the question repeatedly but I could not find an easy answer. She was the only friend I had in the town at that time of hardship. I finally came to the conclusion that I was trying to conceal my 'good intention' towards the baby from her.

It had become a tradition that if there was any misunderstanding between me and Dr. Okon, my wardrobe always increased its intake. That evening he came back home with a new dress for me. It was a costly one and fitted perfectly. He knew my size in dresses and often did not consult me before buying me a dress. This evening when he came back with the new dress in its packet he shouted, "Darling, I have something for you." I did not reply.

I was in the inner room dressing the baby when he appeared, smelling of the fresh air from outside. As I struggled with the safety pin, trying to push it through the napkin, the baby kicked her legs in the air. She was a fine baby; but she resembled her father a little. Those sunken eyes were those of her father. Yet I must not underrate the father himself. He was a handsome man who sported a long, luxuriant beard with a fine moustache that curved down to meet it. He often wore a *'Jews'* with a heavy string of beads to match. His forehead always shone in the dark. For the past ten years he had been a medical doctor working in Murtala Mohammed Hospital at Kano. He came originally from Calabar. "I have something very nice for you, my darling," he whispered into my ear, obviously thinking I had not heard him answer.

I did not give him a word of an answer, neither did I turn my face to look at him. He must have sensed that I was still nursing my anger from the previous day. I dressed the baby and held her against my shoulders as I walked quickly towards the sitting room. As I went along the narrow passage that led from my room to the parlor, I was aware that he was following me closely with the packet in his left hand, pressed tightly to his side. When I reached the parlor, I settled down on the sofa with the baby on my lap. The bruises made by my fingers were still visible on her face.

Dr. Okon came over and took his seat beside me. I began to feel a sense of uneasiness as he sat there. I could feel the warmth of his heavy-built body beside me. The packet containing the dress was still in his hand. Without looking in my direction he asked, "Are you still cross with me over what happened last night? You just have to forget about what happened... I mean the last incident... things like that do happen at times. It was nobody's fault..."

My throat felt dry, but I had to say a word or two to him. I adjusted the position of the baby on my lap, moistened my lips, looked straight into his eyes and asked, "Why did you hit me so much? You wouldn't have done that to me if... Now look... look at the condition of my face! See how swollen it has become. If it is not better by tomorrow, how can you expect me to show my face at work?"

"It was the sight of the baby... It terrified me greatly. I wonder what exactly you did to her. Your excuse was too thin to be true. How could the baby fall out of the cot?" He paused for a moment. "Well, let's forget about what happened." He paused again, thoughtfully. "We shall be having dinner with the family of Dr. Tenga tonight, which is the reason I bought you this." He gently placed the package beside me. Then, moving closer, he attempted to plant a kiss on my lips but I pushed him away. I needed no kiss, no love, nothing from him this evening.

How could he even think of me going to a dinner party in my present condition? Was he not a fool to accept an invitation from Dr. Tenga and his family when he had not consulted me beforehand? As long as I remained in his house I was his 'wife' and he was my 'husband', though I was not legally married to him. I hated the two titles—'wife' and 'husband'—when they referred to my relationship with Dr. Okon. As long as I remained in his house I knew I would hate those things he loved and love those things he hated.

Dr. Tenga came from Zimbabwe. He worked as a medical doctor at the Murtala Mohammed hospital as well. The whole of his family had been good to me. His eldest daughter, Ruth, came frequently to our house. She was a girl of about seventeen, very beautiful, gentle and extra-intelligent. She was a student at the Federal Advanced Teachers' College. Any time she was in Kano on vacation, I was sure of having somebody to keep me company throughout most of the evenings, especially before the baby was born. Whenever I felt really weighed down I would send for her and she would not hesitate to come and comfort me. To me she was like a sister, born of the same parents. This evening, her father had invited us to dine with the family to welcome her home on holiday. That was the way they were. "I'm not going," I said flatly. He brushed down his thick beard with his hand. For a moment he did not speak, just sat with his head bent. "What did you say?" he asked finally. "I said I'm not going to the party," I repeated.

In silence, he stood up, stepped over my wide-spread lap and made his way to the bedroom. He was really an unpredictable sort of a man; I did not understand him. I knew he loved me greatly, yet I had never at any time responded to this love. I could not bring myself to feel any love for him. He was not my man. My man was still in a foreign land receiving treatment from the hands of foreigners.

Dr. Okon was the burden I had to bear for the sake of my real love. All those years with Idu Idoko were not a memory which could be scrapped. I could not forget those years of promise, love and tenderness. Fate had decreed that Idu, my fiancé, should fall victim to an ugly accident. After a long battle to save him from being a paraplegic the doctors had decided that he had more chance of recovery if he could get treatment abroad. Idu had no money of his own and no one to help him. Dr. Okon had come up with the suggestion that he would persuade the Kano State Ministry of Health to take care of everything on the condition that I submit to his love demands. He knew very well that I was Idu's fiancée, and so would do anything I could to save his dear life. Dr. Okon had earlier made a love approach to me, which I had declined. To save my love, however, I had to agree to the man's conditions. I had done so.

The greatest moment of regret in my life came when Idu was leaving the country in the early hours of the morning. I should have remained to see him off, but I failed to do so. That had obviously hurt him as his letter had proved. Was that why he had now decided to marry another girl, a white girl, who did not know the culture of his people? He had thought that I had left him for another man. He had never known the truth. I could not tell him; Dr. Okon had forbidden me to mention it. I knew too, that if anything went wrong with Idu's marriage to the white girl, I would probably be held responsible. You might be wondering why Dr. Okon had remained a bachelor for so long. He was an important and well-thought of man. Perhaps I can show the reasons as I tell my story.

My thoughts were interrupted when he came back to the parlor with a fresh black suit on. He did not even glance at me but moved over to the television set in the parlor. He switched on the set and tuned it to Channel Five, NTV Kano. This channel was showing a Hausa program with the traditional beating of drums and movements of bodies they called dancing. It was not to the taste of a non-Hausa person. With a show of irritation, Dr. Okon reached for the 'off' button.

He stood up, looked at me and then at the sleeping baby. "Are you sure you are not going?"

"No, I'm not going to the party," I told him. "But please tell Ruth to come and see me tomorrow evening. Tell her that I would love to see her."He took out a white handkerchief from his pocket and wiped his mouth with it. "How can you expect her to come here tomorrow when you won't accept a simple invitation from them to dinner tonight?"He left the parlor hurriedly, slamming the door with a deafening bang. The noise made both me and the baby jump. Oh, how can I describe how I felt about him as I saw him moving out of the house alone towards the garage!! He did not know that the 'contract' I had earlier signed with him would soon expire. He knew that very soon I intended to leave him for the one man I had ever loved. I was determined to try all I could to draft a lengthy letter to Idu Idoko that night. I must let him know that everything I had done was to safeguard his health. All I wanted was his happiness. I had not reckoned with Abubakar, his dear friend and my enemy, misinterpreting my actions to Idu. I had not actually seen Abubakar since Idu had left the country, and I wondered how he had got hold of the information about me. It was amazing how fast bad news could travel across the waters! But how could I convince Idu in a letter? I must talk to him in person. He needed to see the tears that could not be shed through the lines the overseas envelope would carry.

Chapter 3

The next day, back at work, while I was attending to a customer, I saw Ruth Tenga with some provisions she had just picked up from the shelves. 'Hi, Ruth,' I called softly, knowing she would recognize my voice. The girl looked up and our eyes met. A look of distaste flashed across her face. I knew it was because of my still swollen face. 'Hello, Madam,' she said, moving closer to me. She did not address me by my personal name. I found that irritating. But as long as I had that baby at home, she would equate me with her own mother, Mrs. Tenga. The moment a girl marries she is given special respect by the rest of the world, no matter what her age is. The moment she is put to bed, she becomes rated among the old women who have long known men. The type of freedom a girl enjoyed when she was single ends automatically when she gets married. It seemed to me that a girl can only enjoy her life before she gets married or has experienced the pain of child-bearing. 'Dr. Okon told me you were back home on holiday.' I stopped what I was doing on the calculating machine and gently took her hands in mine. 'Yes, I'm back home. How is the baby doing?' she asked. 'She is doing fine,' I answered.

'Are you here to do much shopping?' I did not want her to complete her sentence in such a public place in case what I dreaded to hear from her was in fact what she was going to say, so I interrupted. My hands then went back to settle on the calculator keys. My fingers trembled as they struck the keys. 'You must come and see me at our house. How about this evening?' She nodded agreement.

Five-thirty. The working hours were over. That day, when I left work, a guilty conscience followed me closely back home. Had the Tenga family been told what had happened to my daughter? Had Dr. Okon discovered the whole truth behind the bruises on the face of his daughter? I really could not tell.

Disembarking from the taxi cab, I began to feel a sense of dizziness. It was the thought of my daughter lying there, sleeping peacefully in her cot or on Naomi's lap that made me feel sick. How could I go back home now and face her, or kiss her innocent brow, when I knew she had already discovered that I had no love, no motherly love, for her? I knew for sure that her eyes would now look accusingly at me whenever I was near her.

As I went into the house, I met Dr. Okon with a newspaper in his hand. I had no intention of talking to him this evening. In fact, ever since this last incident, I had grown to hate him and even hated the house itself. 'Hi,' I managed to say.'Hello,' he answered with a wave of his hand.

I stumbled across the wide parlor to my bedroom. Ever since the baby had come, I had been sharing this bedroom with nobody except the baby who had her own cot at the side of my bed. I had sworn to myself that I would not allow Okon to share my bed with me until after the baby had reached the age of one. Would I remain in this house with him then, even give birth to another baby for him, the man I could not love? I wondered.

The baby had been fed by Naomi just before I came in. There, she lay on the lap of the little girl who had been trying for some time to get her to sleep. The baby's eyes were half-closed and half-opened, the sleep of a young fish. 'Welcome, Madam.'

'Thank you,' I answered. 'How is the baby doing?' 'She dey fine. I just give her chop and she want to sleep.' In order to put her into a deeper sleep, Naomi started petting her. I moved over to the baby and touched her lightly on the forehead. She reacted sharply to the touch. It appeared she did not like that touch from me. Was she thinking I might make a further attempt to harm her? How could I possibly pull a hair from her head in the presence of this young girl, Naomi? At first, I wondered if the reaction was as a result of some chill generated by my hand. I tested my hand against my cheek to see how cold it was. It was quite warm. My heart began to race.

'Take her to her bed,' I ordered the girl, 'and if you want to go out, lock the door for me. I want to go to sleep. If any person comes looking for me, tell the person I no dey for house. But if na that girl who dey come here every day comes asking of me, come inside my room and call me—that Zimbabwe girl I tell you. You hear me?' 'Yes, Madam.' I went over to the wardrobe, pulled off my dress and went straight to bed. Lying beside me, in her own cot, was the baby who had never at any time sucked my breast. There she lay as a separate being—separate from me and my world. She had her own world which was beautiful and tender. I had my own world which was ugly in thoughts and wicked in deeds. Over and over again, those thoughts kept on flashing in my mind until at last I closed my eyes to the outside world. In a waking sleep, I heard the dry crack of the door opening. It was Naomi coming to wake me up. I opened my eyes and saw her standing at the door. This was so unusual that I was instantly awake. Normally, before coming in for anything, she would have at least given three loud knocks at the door. Something serious must have gone wrong somewhere outside, I thought. 'What is the matter with you, Naomi?' I barked at her fearfully, forgetting to bring my level of English down to meet hers. 'Why have you come crashing in here like this?'

She looked frightened and stood speechlessly by the door as if her tongue had been glued to her upper palate. 'I asked you what was wrong.' I questioned her again as I got out of bed. I felt stupid and embarrassed standing there in front of Naomi. She had never before seen me so nearly naked. 'Na Madam. She... she... don come.' She stammered out her message. Though she had not mentioned the name of the 'Madam' who had just come, I knew that it must be Ruth. 'All right. Make you dey go. Tell her to wait in the parlor for me. I will soon be there.' I tried to sound simple. She smiled at me and left the room with the message, gently closing the door behind her.

I went back to my wardrobe and got out a loose red dress. When I was ready, I went through to the parlor to see Ruth. When she saw me, she smiled with pleasure. I must say again that she was a very beautiful girl, even though it is often very hard for a girl of my age to admit to the beauty of another. She looked more beautiful than I did, I knew. I envied her freedom. She had control of her own life. She neither had a baby nor a rigid man to occupy her mind. She was a free schoolgirl. 'Good evening, Madam,' she said cheerfully.

'Hello, Ruth,' I answered, trying to stifle a yawn. I walked towards her and noticed that sitting opposite her was Dr. Okon dressed in his black *Afe* with his heavy beard resting on his chest. What was he waiting for with those empty eye sockets? I had not expected to see him there. He had never before stayed so long in the house after working hours. He must have been waiting for something special this evening. I decided that he was probably waiting to talk to me in the presence of the girl, Ruth. She was a family friend as well as my best friend in this town. Perhaps he felt that I needed advice from her on something. I could not yet tell, but felt so uneasy that I could not easily keep up a conversation with Ruth in his presence.'Where is the baby?' she asked. 'She is sleeping in the bedroom,' I answered. 'She is fine, em... and how are the other members of the Tenga family doing?'

'Oh, they have all gone out today so they don't know that I've come here,' she laughed, waving her hand. How beautiful those fingers were, dancing in the air; slender fingers, matching her slender figure. 'How long are you on holiday? When did you come here? This week, I imagine.'

'No, last week... To be precise, I came home on Thursday,' she answered. 'It's marvelous to be home. The food is dreadful at the college. The common diet there is eba and beans. Oh, the thought... I really hate the food. It makes me feel sick.' She turned to Dr. Okon. 'Why must we go on eating stone-filled rice in my school?' she asked.

Dr. Okon cleared his throat. 'Let me try to explain things to you, my dear Ruth. The moment you step out of your mother's house, you can no longer expect to eat those delicious foods you have been eating before. You have now become a stranger, taking whatever food comes within the reach of your mouth... The cooks do not purposely pour gravel into the rice provided for the students. But the size of the institution dictates how the food should be prepared, and you can hardly expect such a very large quantity of rice to be cooked without stones, can you?'

Oh, this was too much! Dr. Okon was trying to steer the evening conversation with Ruth away from me. He was so pompous! I could no longer bear to listen to him... to his stupid ideas. How I wished that he had left the house as usual. I made an excuse and left the parlor, leaving him to finish his boring lecture. I would come in later when he had gone, worn out with all that pomposity. Then I would be free to talk to Ruth myself about what interested me. I had not invited her round to discuss matters affecting her and her colleagues in the Federal Advanced Teachers' College!

Thinking that Dr. Okon must have left the parlor, I came back a little later. But he was still there, talking away. When he saw me, he looked at his wrist watch and at last made to pick up the keys of his car from the center table. I sighed. 'Take care of the house,' he murmured to me, jingling the bunch of keys in his hand. 'I shall be back very soon.' I knew at once what was going to happen. Should I allow Ruth to take leave of me so easily? I must make her stay for a while. I turned to her and asked after her boyfriend, Ojo. She smiled. 'That is history now. We are no longer friends.' 'Why? What happened?' I asked, trying to sound serious. I moved closer to her and took her hand in mine. With her free hand, she brushed back her long hair. 'He is an unstable sort of a boy and that was what parted us,' she said.

'But you shouldn't have broken up so easily. After all, you have known each other for a very long time. Everybody thought that you would get wedded to each other eventually. Now, tell me what really happened.' 'It is a long story. But I can tell you that he is a terrible flirt,' she said. 'All men flirt,' I maintained. Dr. Okon cracked the air with his laughter. He was still on his feet, with his left fingers playing with the beads round his neck and his right hand tossing the keys. He tried to defend men. 'Women, women, you are creatures known for flirting!'

Before I had the chance to say another word he moved to the door saying that I should look after the house. 'Sorry to leave you, Madam,' Ruth apologized. 'The doctor is going to drop me at a friend's house. I promised to meet her at her house by six-thirty this evening. Perhaps I could come and see you again tomorrow evening? About this time?' 'Yes, yes, I'll see you again,' I said flatly. Frustration appeared to be creeping into every part of my life. Who needed her to call again, anyway? I asked myself. With my eyes hard, I watched them take leave of the parlor. My head felt heavy above my shoulders.

I collapsed into the cushion chair. It was not that I hated Ruth going out with the doctor. The fact was that, through a feeling of depression, frustration and loneliness, I had invited the girl to keep me company that evening. I had thought that I might possibly be able to tell her some of my problems. Yet, with a pitiless mind, Dr. Okon had emerged from an unknown place and had snatched her from me. Could it be that that was why he had refused to leave the house all the evening? There, in the cushion chair, I lay out plotting and planning. Why should all this happen to me?

Chapter 4

Outside, the harmattan wind was blowing. Inside my room it was so cold that my skin was covered in goose-pimples. I could not imagine sleeping alone in this cold, silent house. Apart from Naomi, and the helpless little baby lying peacefully in her cot, the house was without a soul. At midnight, I longed for the presence of Idu to warm up the chilly bed for me. But he was not there. He was in a distant land unknown to me. He could only be drawn to my room with the help of dreams.

Only God knew when Dr. Okon would be back home tonight. He had left home at six-thirty and now it was midnight, yet he was not back home. This particular residential area was so far removed from the city-world that, once it was about eight in the evening, one might be forgiven for doubting the existence of any other living souls there. Inspired by this loneliness, I decided to write a lengthy letter to Idu. He must be told about my feelings for him and that he had the wrong idea of my staying with Dr. Okon. I had to tell him that Abubakar's information about me was a lie. Idu must be made to realize that all Abubakar had done was to set us apart for reasons best known to him. All these misconceptions would have to be cleared up in this letter.

Sleep had already started gathering over the hem of my eyebrows. But I was determined that nothing should stop me from writing the letter that night. My fingers felt heavy as I moved to pick up the pen that lay on top of the dressing table. I looked over to where my baby lay in her cot, her thumb in her mouth. She had no other personal problems at all except me. I knew she had no confidence in me. I reached for my writing pad, settled down on the bed and began to write the letter on my lap. At first, I had some difficulties about how to start the letter. Choosing the opening words took me almost twenty minutes. At last, I started to write it.

Dear Idu,

I got your letter on the 26th of last month. Thank you very much for it. I was surprised to hear from you after all these months of separation. I'm not talking about separation in love but separation by distance. I would have written to you before but I did not know your address. I really thank God that you have been brought back to your natural health and will be coming back to Nigeria very soon. I could hardly believe my eyes when I read the wonderful news.

Idu, I cannot hide the fact that you have really broken my heart with that ugly letter you wrote to me. Can you really believe that I could do the things you say? I know I'm a woman, but women are not the same everywhere. I just can't imagine how such a dubious character as Abubakar can come between you and I and set us apart. You must know my love for you stands as firm as a strong rock under the harsh weather. You often tried to shake my love for you, but you never succeeded. I loved you too much.

It is true that I'm now staying with Dr. Okon—you know him very well. And the person who told you that must by this time also have told you that I have had a baby girl for him. I'm sure you will hear many things about me which will later prove to be either true or false. There are also a good many things that I want to tell you concerning Dr. Okon, but I cannot write them in a letter. I can only tell you when we are together again—if ever we do meet again. You must realize that all that I have done was for your own good. This was the only way for you to get out of this country, to go abroad for treatment. There was no other way. I promise you that very soon Dr. Okon will get out of my way.

Idu, surely you can't have forgotten about the cock-crows you called the darkness of the night? You must remember that night of togetherness when everything and everywhere was completely quiet except for the occasional interruption from a hooting owl, and the attacking mosquitoes. That was the wonderful black night when you said you loved me dearly and promised me a wedding ring as soon as possible. How could we know that you would be involved in that dreadful road accident and that everything would be brought to a stand-still? Idu, Idu, think how you introduced me to your parents. Remember that they are expecting me to become their daughter-in-law one day. They still believe that you are coming back home to marry me.

If I have wronged you in any way, can't you just forgive me rather than rushing straight into the arms of a foreigner, a stranger? She doesn't know the origins, the customs or the culture of your people. When you are sick she will not take any proper care of you. When you die she will run away with your children to the land where your parents will see them no more. Think about all these things before you take another step. You only have to forgive and forget my mistakes. After all, I forgave you when you once did me wrong by taking Amina as your girlfriend when you were still in Kano. I know perfectly well that you must be feeling as lonely there as I am here in this ugly house. The feminine body of the white girl cannot keep you warm but that of your African love can. As far as I know, your parents are doing fine. Your mother is gradually regaining her sight. The erection of her building that you started, but did not finish before you left on that fateful day, has now been completed by your dear enemy, Abubakar. I call him your enemy because he is out to deprive you of me. And did you know that he has gone and married Amina? What do you think about that?

As soon as you get this letter, please try to write to me and tell me the very day you will be landing again on the soil of your own people. I am prepared to go and welcome you at the airport in sorrow even if I cannot do it in happiness. Oh, Idu! How I wish you had seen me before taking this final decision!

Ever yours, Onyemowo Adum

By the time I had finished drafting the letter, it was very late because it had taken me almost an hour to finish. The baby rolled over on to her side in her cot and began to cry deafeningly. She was probably hungry. She would have to be fed before she would take another hour of sleep. I dragged my feet towards her and picked her up in my arms. The food had already been prepared. She usually woke in the night, so I had taken the precaution of preparing the food beforehand. I must feed her. Yes, I must fatten her like the special cow ready for the right time. She was really hungry. My daughter gulped down the contents of the feeding bottle, then resumed her sleep. Gently, gently, I placed her back in her cot.

I looked at the letter again and tidied it up a little. What remained to be done now was to address the envelope. I could give it to the mail runner at Leventis first thing in the morning when I got to work. It ought to be addressed ready.

I took a long stride to fish the address out from under my pillow. But... What...? I could not believe my eyes when I discovered that the letter I had received from Idu was no longer there. In a rage, I flung the soft pillow over my head. It flew in the air and narrowly missed the cot in which my baby lay. Where on earth had the letter gone? Who on earth had come to my bedroom to make away with the letter? I then proceeded with the search for it by crawling under my bed to see if it had fallen on the floor. But, apart from my brassiere which lay forlornly in a corner, the floor was as tidy as the surface of the full-grown moon. I rushed over to the heavy box that stood at the end of my bed, to check if it might be there. How could I post this letter in my hand to Idu without the address? How? How? I found that I could not cry out. Only the chilly tears could be felt rushing down over my nose.

I was still there, kneeling at the foot of the bed crying when a knock struck at the window that led to my bedroom. I knew it must be Dr. Okon coming back home after the long hours of staying outside the house. It couldn't be the little girl, Naomi, who slept in the parlor. She was a heavy sleeper and no amount of knocking on the door could stir her to life. Naomi couldn't be the perpetrator of that continuous and heavy knocking. Dr. Okon always knocked at my window any night he happened to come back home very late from the drinking parlors; late from where free women plied the roads around the Central Hotel; home with his clothes stinking of liquor and strange bodies.

It was already after one. Why should I go and open that door for him? Let him go back where he had come from. Let him go back to Ruth. I was now suspicious of his frequent outings in the day and his coming back home late at night. Why shouldn't I grow suspicious? Ruth had been home for some time and I had often used the same excuse as she had given me that night, before escaping with him. The knocking was repeated on and on. Then a voice came through the closed window.

"Please, open the door for me, my dear." Though the window was securely locked from inside, I could smell the stale, stinking beer coming from outside and gathering around my nose. There was also something strange about his voice. Ever since Dr. Okon had caught me red-handed in the attempt to murder my baby, he had found it very difficult to pronounce the word, 'dear' when talking to me. I had not had a single warm kiss from his lips either. In that cold room, kneeling below the window and trying to control my flowing tears, I knew that he wanted to kiss me if only I would be willing to let him in.

"For goodness sake, open that door for me," the voice came again, but this time it was more authoritative. Then it gradually began to lose its force. "Please, allow me in. I want to talk to you."

"I do not want to hear any more of your talking!" I stormed. "You can do all the talking to yourself. Do it outside there, or go back to that girl and do it with her!" For some seconds there was silence. Then he asked quietly, "Which girl are you talking about?" "Do you really expect me to...?"

"I just want to know which particular girl you are referring to. Does that explain why you are refusing to let me in? Do you really imagine that a full-bodied, grown-up man like myself should stay all day and all night long with a woman who... who... I'm sorry, onyemowo, but it is not very long since you had your baby!"

"I don't want to hear more about it, is that clear?" I interrupted. In fact, I was not in the mood to argue about anything with him. All I was after now, the only thing that was in my mind, was Idu's address. Why should Okon steal it from me? What was he going to do with it? Was he going to make use of it by writing to Idu in a bid to soil my name? And if he wanted to do that, why had he waited until this time before doing so?

"Where is that letter you stole from under my pillow!" I asked tactlessly. "Letter?" He sounded genuinely puzzled. "Are you asking me if I have stolen a letter of yours?" "Tell me where you've put the letter." As I spoke, my voice trembled. "What on earth would I want a letter of yours for?" "Do you mean to tell me that you did not take my letter from my room?"

The baby moved in the cot. Was my daughter going to blame me for the accusations I was making about her father tonight? If she wanted to start crying again tonight, she would have to cry alone. I wasn't prepared to comfort her, to beg her to keep quiet, and she knew it. I went to the window, opened it slightly and leant against the glass.

"I don't know anything about your letter! Let me in. I want to discuss something in connection with our baby with you. Do you understand me?" His voice was pleading. The cold outside was obviously affecting him. What did he want to discuss with me about our baby? Why must that discussion be held this very night, after he had tired himself in some joint only known to him, and not any other night? My heart began to race. Had he forgotten about what happened between me and the baby? "All right!" I snapped. "You may come in and say whatever you wish to say to me." I went towards the door, opened it and waited for him to come in. The car was already parked in the garage at the front of the house.

I stood there waiting on the threshold in the cold, but he did not show his face at the door. What the hell was he waiting for now? Had he come home with a woman and was he having a tough time persuading her to step into the house? I could not find the answer. It was one-thirty in the morning. I decided to go and check the back of the house before I finally went back to bed. I stepped out of the house. A neighboring dog barked and I shivered with cold and fright. There was no other sound—not even the laughter of the crickets.

Oh! In vomit! In urine! Dr. Okon lay on the infant grass at the back of the house just below my window, smelling revolting. Sleeping, stinking doctor! He had never done this before. Never, never in his lifetime had he done this! I just could not believe my eyes. What had he been doing?

"What have you done?" I asked him. I did not touch him as he lay on the grass, but stood away, far away, as if he had a deadly and communicable disease.

He raised up his head and, without opening his eyes, said, "Where is... my woman? I need my woman. Ruth... get me another glass of wine. I need wine. I need my woman." With my hands under his armpits I dragged his inert body to the house and left him on the bare floor. He would have to lie there until morning, I said to myself.

Chapter 5

A week after that night when the doctor had come home in that revolting state, talking about his imaginary women, the moment I had long been waiting for arrived. It was six in the evening. I had already eaten after the long hours of work in the Leventis Stores and was relaxing by the television set, watching a program and at the same time feeding my baby. Dr. Okon suddenly called out to me.

'Onyemowo!' 'Yes,' I answered. 'How was the day's work?' he asked, coming in and sitting down. 'Fine.'

He had never before asked me about my work. I began to wonder why he was behaving in such a strange manner. I was sure that he was trying to dig something out of me with these tactics. For a week now, we had been like two strangers living under the same roof, with nothing in common. 'I hear that you have been promoted,' he said. 'Where did you hear that?' 'Do you want to hide it from me?' he asked, smiling gently.

'What do you think I am trying to hide from you?' The food I was giving to the baby spilled onto my dress and I quickly brushed it off to avoid leaving a stain. I thought back to what had happened. I had not referred to it during the day because I knew he would be angry. In fact, I had hardly seen him alone since I had left him lying on the floor. Our conversation tonight seemed to be all questions. 'I have been told that you are having a secret love affair with the top man you are working under and that that is what has led to your recent promotion in the office. Is that true?' I was astounded and could not answer at once.

'Onyemowo, I would like us to take a little walk outside the house,' he said calmly. One of the favorable qualities I found in Dr. Okon, if I am honest, was his manner of talking. He was not a man of many words. He had never liked dragging words about and ending up saying precisely nothing. But what he was trying to say now was not really true. It was true enough that I had been promoted from the grade level 05 to level 06, and was now working in the executive office of the firm, but it was not true that all this was as a result of what he referred to as a secret love affair with my boss. I had never told him anything about my promotion, so I wondered exactly who on earth had told him all these stories about me.

We walked out into the garden pushing the little baby in the perambulator. The gardener was there, very busy tilling the soil in the beautiful flower beds. He was now a white-haired old man without a single tooth in his mouth. He had been a gardener to Dr. Okon for a long time before I arrived on the scene. His story was very sad. He hardly ever mentioned anything about it. His whole family had been killed one morning during a heavy downpour in Kano. The house in which his family of seven were living had been brought down by the rainfall and they had all been buried. He himself had not been in the house when the tragedy had happened. When the news about what happened to his family had reached his ears, he had threatened to take his own life but friends had looked after him and had dissuaded him from this action. He was a sad, patient man.

We lived in the Nassarawa residential area of the city. This is an area reserved for the top officials of the government only, or so it seemed. In fact, the people who lived there were all rich and well-known. Our house was some way from the main road. Walking slowly, we headed for the main road. As we passed the gardener, Dr. Okon asked me to wait a moment. I stopped and adjusted the position of the belt around my waist. In those tight trousers, I felt smart and quite masculine and chic. 'I have been wanting to talk to you,' he declared. 'About what?' I asked with my eyes searching for shadows in the empty air. The accusation he had made about me before we left the house was still burning in my heart. 'You are as aware as I am that our relationship in this house has not been cordial. We have not been feeling that sense of...'

'Is that why you asked me to come out?' I interrupted, looking him straight in the eyes. 'I can no longer continue to lead this type of life, a life of having to put up with insinuations from friends and relatives. I want to marry you publicly and in a formal way. Many times I have thought of throwing you out of this house and out of my life...' 'And why didn't you do it?' I interrupted again. 'Because of the baby, our daughter. I need our daughter. And if you went now, who would take care of the baby? I need to marry and settle down as a responsible man; responsible in the eyes of my colleagues. Yes, I want to be a man of standing in society.'

The light breeze blew the sand off the ground and blew it in my face. I quickly turned my face away, whirling the baby round to face the direction we had come in order to protect her from the attack of the harmattan wind. 'But any woman you married as your wife would surely take care of your baby for you. On several occasions, I have told you that the only man for me is Idu. What has happened already will not stop me from marrying him,' I asserted. By this, I was referring of course to the pregnancy and the unfortunate birth of this baby I was pushing before me. 'Ever since he left the country, has he written you a single letter?' Dr. Okon asked. 'He has written to me.'

'What did he write in the letter?'

'You should know, you stole it!'

'Did I?'

'Who else do you think would come into my bedroom and make away with it? I have written a letter of reply telling him to go ahead with his marriage with the white lady and that I'm now happily settled down with you. But how could I post the letter without his address? How could I post it when you refused to give the address back to me?'

He did not say a word and I thought he was probably weighing up my previous statements about my firm love for Idu and this sudden change of heart.

'I need that address from you, Doc,' I said again. 'Did he say he was going to marry a white girl?' he asked, stroking his beard. 'Didn't you read the letter?' I asked. 'And do you mean to tell him all this?' I will tell him everything if only you will give me back the letter. I really mean to do it,' I lied. Was my ruse going to work? I wondered. He bent down and kissed the little baby in the perambulator on the forehead. The baby smiled back at him. This might be the last kiss she received from Dr. Okon, I thought.

'Onyemowo, we shall celebrate her naming ceremony next week. I would like you to make a full preparation for this occasion. It is going to be a big occasion...' 'Naming ceremony! She is too old now for us to celebrate her name! We should have done this much earlier. She is now almost five months old.'

'Ha, ha, ha!!' laughed Dr. Okon. 'This is my baby, my daughter, and until now she has had no name. Is this not ridiculous? Do you want us to continue calling her "Baby"? It isn't really funny. On the contrary, it is really sad.' He shook his head, sounding serious. 'She is my daughter and I want her to have a name. We shall invite the Minister of Health to be the chairman of the occasion. I'm sure you'll want to invite all your friends to the party.

Please do so. What name do you suggest we should give to her?' I did not answer. 'Don't you want our baby to have a name?' 'Why are you so concerned about her having a name?' I asked.

'Onyemowo, why did your parents choose to give you the very name you are bearing?' I thought over this for a while; I searched for an answer to it but could not find it. At last I said, 'I don't know.' 'Then you must not ask me why our baby should be given a name. Now what name do you have in mind for the baby?' 'Any name at all,' I said. 'What about "Onye-Okon"?'

'Ha, hi, hi!' I giggled at the formulation of the name. 'Funny of you. Ha, ha, ha...' 'What is so funny about the name?' he snapped. 'With this name, neither of us will be cheated because it is a combination of your name and my name. Or don't you understand the whole idea very well?' I merely laughed in reply. I patted him on the back. All the way back to the house, we held each other's hands, laughing heartily as we went along; going past the gardener, we laughed, but the old man was not distracted from his work. He seemed not to pay any attention to us as we went along with the baby sharing our laughter. He was so busy working and caring for the flowers that he probably never noticed.

All he had now were the flowers he was tending so carefully. He no longer had a wife, just the flowers surrounding the house. A new life had been born into the family of Dr. Okon and myself and the old man was hardly aware of it. It might have seemed that love was beginning to blossom between us. But it wasn't so. I had made my plan and knew how to carry it out; nobody was going to be allowed to change or spoil it. I must not stop the race until the baby and Dr. Okon had gone out of my life. In the sky, over the east, the thick, black clouds were gathering. Was it going to rain? In the heart of the harmattan, it would be very strange. Everything that had happened today was strange. Dr. Okon looked up at the clouds. 'Is it going to rain?' he asked. I smiled.

Chapter 6

At eleven-thirty that night, a real drama for Dr. Okon and I took place. After I had put the baby to sleep and had just gone to bed myself, Dr. Okon appeared in my room wearing only his pajamas. For a long time now, since before the baby's birth in fact, he had not come to my room dressed like that. As I have said before, I would not have welcomed any desire on his part to make love to me while the baby was so young. I would not have another pregnancy in that house, I had vowed to myself. But here he was, his hands in the pockets of the pajamas, walking gently towards the bed on which I lay, lips curved in a smile. 'You haven't been to sleep yet?' he said, sitting down on the edge of the bed. 'I was sleeping but you came and woke me up,' I lied. 'Sorry.' I did not answer.

He bent over and put his right arm around my waist. I pushed it aside. He gave a little laugh and brought it round again, then started caressing the inner part of my left thigh. I enjoyed it, but pretended I hated it right to the bottom of my heart. Yet why shouldn't I have taken delight in his loving touch? After all, it had been a long time since I had felt such a manly body against mine. But I was determined not to allow him to plant another seed inside me. He leaned over and kissed me on my mouth. I liked that too, but when he started digging his hand into my nightdress, I held his hand back. 'No! Don't try it,' I protested. 'Don't you know that our baby is still young?'

He took no notice and I knew perfectly well what he was after. If he would not stop it willingly, I must then force him to stop it against his will. If he was here to force me, then I would tell him plainly that I was not the type of girl to let him get away with it easily. Dr. Okon's behavior that night reminded me of what happened when Idu was still in the Murtala Mohammed Hospital in Kano. I had gone to the hospital to pay him a visit one afternoon. Dr. Okon had met me in the hospital ward and had called me to his office. When we got there, he had pretended to talk to me about Idu, almost as if I were his next-of-kin. But matters had soon taken another turn. Something terrible had happened and it was this that was now at the root of my attitude towards him.

As he did not seem willing to stop, I started to struggle with him. Bathed in hot sweat, I kicked him hard with my legs. 'The deer is tired and the dog also is tired,' is a popular saying among my people. At last, I perceived that his very manhood had begun to desert him. I could see signs of tiredness in him. I felt tired too. 'I will buy you whatever you want in the morning only if you could let me... just tonight,' he begged me, as he lay in submission.

Then the idea of the missing address flashed into my mind. This was the perfect time to get the address from him if he really was the person who had taken that letter I had kept under my pillow. If he had it with him, I knew he would be only too willing to hand it over to me then. One thing was certain and that was unless he was fully satisfied with the whole thing tonight, he would not leave my bed. 'I would like one thing from you,' I said. 'What is that?' he asked. 'I want that letter from you.'

He hesitated, then said, 'But I did not take that letter from you and I have already told you so.' 'I want to have the address from you,' I repeated. He pulled his left hand out from under my body and scratched his forehead. I knew he wanted to take his time about whatever he did that night, so that he did not regret anything afterwards. 'All right, all right. I will give it to you in the morning,' he said finally.

'No! I need it now so that I can address the letter in the morning for posting,' I protested. He then said he would let me have access to it that very night after the love-making. But I refused to give in to him until he gave the letter to me. I was aware of the fact that the price I was prepared to pay in order to get Idu's address could be a heavy one. I knew I was risking my life and happiness by agreeing to his terms. But there was no choice for me. I had made no preparations for I had never thought that he would demand anything from me while the baby was so young. I had no pills and I was worried about the effects of his demands.

As he left the room, promising to collect it from his room and come back to me, I wondered if he really was the one who had stolen it from me. What reason could he have had for doing so? At last, he came back with a printed address in his right hand. But it wasn't the one that had been at the top of the letter that I had received from Idu. 'Here you are,' he said and handed it over to me.'But this is not the letter,' I pointed out, squeezing up my face as I scrutinized the address. 'I told you that I had not taken it,' he maintained. 'But I did not believe your words,' I said. He shrugged, as if to say that he did not care whether I believed him or not.

At last, I had to agree with him that he had not taken the letter and that I had probably misplaced it somewhere in a corner of my room. In my hand lay the address of Idu Idoko. So why should I bother myself further about the letter? Now I had the address I was free to post the week-old letter to the hospital where my 'fiancé' was receiving treatment. In my room, we both slept until the next morning.

Chapter 7

It was Sunday afternoon. The mist that had earlier gathered in the morning air had been burned away by the sun. White dust had settled on people's hair making them look like old men and women overnight. It was the time when cold-blooded animals were no longer in their hide-outs, trying to conserve their warmth. Evidence of this could be seen in those lizards who jumped from one tree to another outside in the garden. This afternoon I had nothing to do in the house. In order to pass the slow-moving time, I went out to talk to the old man. I often went to him for a chat or to ask about the traditions of our people. Sometimes I would help him water the flowers. We had developed a close relationship and he had grown to look upon me almost as a daughter.

From the old man, I had learned a great deal of the Hausa language and communication with him became easier. I was out there in the garden, discussing the incident of the dusty air about two years ago which had almost brought total darkness to the entire Northern states, when Dr. Okon suddenly appeared. I frowned at his coming to interrupt us. He was always like that. Any time I had a little time at my disposal to talk with people it seemed he would come and put in a blocking stone, and that would end everything. It was three weeks since Ruth had called at my place to keep me company and he had come around and plucked her out of the house; that was the night he had come home late and drunk. This afternoon he was again going to ask the gardener to leave me alone. But he came to me instead. 'I have just been round to see the family of Tenga.'

'Are they doing fine?' I asked, trying to smile for him, covering my anger.

'There was no trouble when I left them.' 'Have you informed them about the naming ceremony of our baby? They will need to know about it in time.' He remained quiet. I continued, 'The people who will be invited to the party need to be informed about it a month or so before the time comes...' 'I have changed my mind about it,' he interrupted. 'About what?' I asked. 'About the naming ceremony. After... Mrs. Tenga wants to see you this evening, at her house.' He suddenly changed the subject. After what? After when? What was he talking about? But I did not ask him. I did not like to bother him with many questions—questions that might lead to uproar in that house. 'I hope nothing serious has happened to the family,' I observed.

'Em... No, no. She just wants to see you, to discuss things with you, women matters, I expect,' he said, stammering a little.

Women matters! I thought. Why women matters? I was not a woman. I was a girl spoiled by a bachelor and forced to take that title that I hated. I intended to change it; it was only a matter of time. Very soon nobody would be able to meet me on the road and point at me exclaiming, 'Hey, look at that woman!' Time changes the face of many things, and what I needed most now was time. To time I owed my life. 'I will go and see her,' I said. 'Well, make sure you don't stay too long there. Have you noticed that Naomi is not very well? I have just given her some drugs. Or will you go along with the baby?'

'Oh, I will go with the baby. She is not too heavy if I push her along in her pram. I will come back in no time.' From our house to Tenga's flat was a distance of one kilometer. With the baby before me in her pram, I could cover the distance without much pain. The road between the two flats was not a busy one so there was not much traffic.

I left the garden, left the old man, went to my room and got dressed up. I then redressed the baby and gently placed her in her perambulator. I took a good look at the baby as I placed her in the pram. She was growing fast. But would she live to see that day when she would stagger about, trying to take her first steps? She was a carbon copy of me and bore little resemblance to her father. Dr. Okon was black in complexion and she was light. She was beautiful and light in complexion and the father was not all that handsome. I, however, was beautiful and light in complexion.

I found Naomi lying on the floor of the parlor. Oh, she looked so pretty! I did not need to disturb her from her blissful sleep. She had complained earlier of stomach troubles and Dr. Okon had just given her some drugs to cool her down. Now she was on the floor with her eyes closed, hands resting over her belly.

As I settled down with Mrs. Tenga in the parlor, one of the girls in the family brought me a cool bottle of ginger ale. I admired the little four-year-old as she bent down with the small bottle opener in her hand, trying to open the ginger ale. I had a vision of the future of my baby, if she had any future at all. 'Fine girl,' I pulled her leg. 'That is enough. I will do the rest of the work myself.'

I took the bottle from her and, putting it to my lips, I took a sip. As the first drop went down my gullet, the girl smiled, then disappeared into one of the bedrooms. 'Ruth!' I called out loudly. Any time I was in that house and I needed her presence I had never asked any member of the family to call her for me, instead I would shout her name. 'Ruth!' I called again.

'Ruth is not in. She has just gone with her father to make some arrangements for her trip back to our own country,' said Mrs. Tenga. 'When is she going back? What is she going to do there? Schooling?' I asked. 'She is only going to spend the Christmas holiday with my old mother there. She will be back before the school opens. Oh, we have some pineapples in the refrigerator. I'm sure you would like a piece of one,' she suggested, and dragged her fat body towards the direction of the refrigerator.

Mrs. Tenga was a Zimbabwean, a lecturer in the Bayero University in Kano. Recently, she had gained her Masters Degree in Mathematics. Oh, what a determined woman she was! What an industrious woman she had proved herself to be! She was the only woman I had ever known who had been awarded a Masters Degree in Mathematics. She was proud of the honor. Unless you heard her speak, which she rarely did, when she spoke in excellent English, you would probably have doubted whether she had ever attended a secondary school. She was a tall woman with a fat body and, until she opened her mouth, you would have said she was no different from any other local woman working in a smoke-infested hut in a remote area of the village. Her thick lips held in them words of wisdom borrowed from both home and abroad.

She soon came back with a bowl of pineapple slices in her hand. As she placed it on the small table beside the cushion chair in which I sat, she came forward and took the baby from my lap. The baby whimpered softly.

'While you eat we can talk, Mrs. Okon—I hope you don't mind me calling you that?' she asked with raised eyebrows. 'No, if that is what you want, I don't mind,' I said, starting to suck and eat the pineapple. 'But I'd prefer you to address me by my personal name, which is Onyemowo, rather than Mrs. Okon. This is because we are not yet legally married.'

'Yes. Exactly, exactly. That really is the purpose of my calling you here this afternoon, Onyemowo,' she said, then paused. 'Is it not high time that you and Dr. Okon were legally and formally married?' 'Oh, as we are now, are we not married to each other? I mean, Dr. Okon and I are leading a married life. Is there no marriage relationship between the two of us as of now?'

She smiled and thought over the question for a while before answering. 'In the context of Nigerian tradition, for two people to be legally married there must be a bride price paid by the suitor to the parents of the girl. And I understand that this has not yet happened between you and Dr. Okon.' With a handkerchief, Mrs. Tenga tidied up the nose of my baby who was busy playing on her lap. 'And who told you that this has not yet happened?'

'Look, Onyemowo. Dr. Okon loves you, and he wants to marry you legally so that you will be his completely. He wants you to have confidence in whatever he does as a husband. He wants you to feel like a wife. You are still young, Onyemowo. You need education. With him you will get that. You will be a lucky girl if you accept my advice and marry him. Dr. Okon needs you...'

'But it is not a question of him needing me. It is a question of a happy marriage,' I interrupted. 'As we are at present, we are happy, and happy to remain like this.' 'Are you really happy?' 'Of course, we are happy,' I affirmed.

A little silence fell in the parlor. Soon after this short silence, Mrs. Tenga spoke again in a cool voice. 'Tell me, Onyemowo, are you really happy to remain a single girl for the rest of your life and never think of attaching yourself to any man?'

'Let me explain something to you,' I said. 'I'll try to be as brief as possible. I'm an Idoma by tribe. Our custom does not permit or accept an illegal child, an illegitimate child. I have already violated this tradition. Yes, Dr. Okon has made me step outside the bounds of my people's culture. Among my people, if a girl gives birth to an illegal child, she is immediately rejected. If the parents receive any money from the man who put her in the family way, the girl will either die or her illegitimate child will die in the process of... I do not want to die, nor do I wish my baby an early death... Do you understand me, Madam?'

'I understand you, my dear,' she said, nodding her head, looking expectantly at me, hoping to hear more. I inclined my head, meaning that I had no more to say about my people and their customs. She looked disappointed. 'It is really hard for the girls in your area,' she commented. 'Is there no other way out?' 'There's nothing we can do except to remain as we are.'

I could see that she was convinced. She did not understand the customs of my people and so anything I told her was bound to sound like the whole truth. 'Dr. Okon told me that you were engaged to a Mr. Idu who is now receiving treatment overseas. How are you going to tackle that problem when the customs of your people do not allow you to take a husband?''I can no longer marry him. The doctor has already marred my plans with Idu. I have already chosen to remain with Dr. Okon forever.'

'But don't you think that there is more prestige in married life than in remaining a single girl for the rest of your life? Marriage is a fine thing.''I agree that married life is better, but there is nothing I can do to make rights out of wrongs,' I said, looking at the floor lest she should read my thoughts. Mrs. Tenga looked closely at the baby and then turned her gaze on me. Her expression was sympathetic. I knew she was worried about my lifestyle. I had finished sucking the pineapple slices. Mrs. Tenga raised her voice and called one of her daughters to come and take the dirty bowl away.

The Tengas had six children and only one of them was a boy. I liked them all. They were beautiful children and all of them were devoted to the boy. Mrs. Tenga was very relaxed with the children and joked and laughed all the time with them in the house.

It was getting on towards six o'clock and I needed to be home in time to prepare the evening meal. Naomi was still ill and could not go to the kitchen to prepare the dinner for the family. I wondered if she was still lying there on the floor where I had left her. She had never been sick before, not since she came to our house. The more I thought of her lying down there on the floor, the more I pitied her. How I wished I could have put myself in her place to bear that sickness instead of her; it did not seem fair that such a tender, flower-like creature should have to bear it alone. The more I imagined her lying on her belly on the floor like a young lizard, helpless, the greater the intensity of my love for her became. What a beautiful girl she was! Once, when I questioned her about her tribe and her parents, she had told me that she came from Calabar and that she was a distant relation of Dr. Okon.

She also explained to me that Dr. Okon had taken her from her home with the intention of getting her into school and bringing her up, or so she was told. When she came to his house, however, she discovered that there was no school for her. On the floor there, she must be very hungry herself, I thought. Dr. Okon would soon be leaving the house. However I felt about him, I never liked to think of him leaving home with an empty stomach. So I made my excuses ready to go back to them.

'We have enjoyed your visit,' Mrs. Tenga smiled. 'I hope everything works out all right for you. Perhaps I ought to talk to Dr. Okon for you. Are you sure that you can't wait to share our dinner with us? Our cook is already in the kitchen preparing it.' 'No, thank you. My house girl is sick. She complains of stomach trouble. By now I'm sure she must be hungry as well as Dr. Okon. This evening they are all depending on me,' I said. 'Express my sympathy to her,' she said. 'I will do it,' I agreed.

I gently put the baby back in her perambulator and off we set back to our own house. Mrs. Tenga walked half the way with us before she finally waved us 'good night'.

Chapter 8

From a distance, I could see Baba, the old gardener, sitting among the flower beds, his withered cheeks buried in his palms. He must be feeling very tired after that long and tedious day in the garden, I guessed. With my little baby over my shoulders, I walked towards him. I was home from work for a few hours.

As I came closer to him, I saw that he was in pain. He was rubbing his right foot with a trembling hand. I went up to him, bent down and touched him lightly on the shoulders and asked what was the matter with him.

Baba looked up and our eyes met. Despite the cold wind blowing fiercely on his face, he was sweating profusely. I was horrified by what I saw— his usual healthy-looking complexion was a deadly color. 'What's happened? Are you in great pain, Baba?' I asked.

He did not answer, even when I repeated the question. 'Baba! Speak to me!' I said loudly. 'It is the snake,' he said at last. At the mention of the word 'snake,' I jumped backward with the baby, as if I had seen it myself. I felt I could feel its presence in the garden. 'What happened to it...? Has it bitten you, Baba?' I asked nervously, bending down to examine his leg.

To this, he replied that a cobra had attacked him as he was weeding the flowerbed, and had bitten him. He also said that he was too weak to run after it with a stick as it slithered away from him after the bite. So the snake had escaped unharmed.

'A cobra!' I exclaimed. I could not allow the old man to die if I could help it. He was the only reliable, the only good friend I had in that house. For this reason alone, I must do all that was within my power to see that he survived the bite from the snake. There was no time to waste. Dr. Okon was not in the house. He was still at work in the hospital. The whole responsibility was mine. I ran to the main road to call a taxi cab to convey the old man to the hospital. Why should the snake attack a peaceful old man? He had never been wicked to any living thing. I was gripped with fear when the old man refused to be taken to the hospital for treatment. For several minutes, both I and the taxi driver stood by the gate, trying to convince Baba to agree to being taken to the hospital. His life must be saved.

'Life? Ha, ha, ha!' Despite the pain he was experiencing, Baba managed a dry laugh. 'For the past ten years has anybody considered me alive? I'm no longer afraid to die. I'm already a dead man...' He paused, then looked into my eyes. 'My daughter, you should not worry yourself about whether I die or not. To me death is not something to be feared but something to be welcomed with an open hand. But for you, I'm worried...'

'Please Baba,' I pleaded, with my hands under his armpits, trying to move him from where he sat. 'If you are really worried about me, then you must consider your own life... you are...'

'Well, Madam, I think I must go on my way,' interrupted the taxi man who was standing behind me in his agbada. I took a sharp look at him and poured out my feelings in angry words. 'Have you no human feelings? Have you no aged father like this old man in your house?' 'But I think I have done my best to persuade him to get into the taxi, but he just refuses. What else do you want me to do, Madam? If you had not brought me here, I would have earned a great deal of money by now.'

There seemed nothing else I could say or do in order to change the taxi man's mind. In view of this, I switched my attention back to the old man. To my surprise, just before the taxi driver could drive away, he willingly got up on his feet without me asking him to do so and got into the taxi. I was anxious to get him to Dr. Okon for treatment as soon as possible.

The telephone in the parlor rang, jerking me from sleep. It was one o'clock in the morning. The door to Dr. Okon's room banged and I heard quick footsteps making their way towards the parlor. I knew it was Dr. Okon and he was going to answer the ringing. It was bound to be some patient or friend calling him to attend to some member of their family in pain, I thought. At first, I didn't think that the call might be from the hospital to which Baba had been admitted earlier in the day. As the idea occurred to me that the call might be from the staff nurse who was attending to the old man in the hospital, I quickly pulled myself out of bed and dragged my shivering feet down to the parlor to meet Dr. Okon.

I reached the parlor just as he was replacing the receiver. He looked worried as he hurried from where the telephone lay. His bald head shone in the dimly-lit parlor as he retied the band around the waist of his pajamas. 'Who rang?' I asked him. 'The call

came from the hospital. The old man is terribly sick...
Now, please look after the house. I must go right
away,' he said, running down the passage that led to
his room. 'I would like to go with you.'

'I told you to look after the house. I will ring
you if anything happens to him,' he called from his
room.

Sleep could no longer gather in my eyes. At
every creak of the wall, my heart jumped or increased
the rate of its beating. I sat on the table on the top of
which the telephone lay motionless. One hour came
and went; still the telephone did not ring. At last, my
eyes began to grow heavy. I tried hard to prevent
myself from falling asleep, but I began to lose the
battle. I placed my head gently on the desk and fell
asleep. Scarcely had my eyes closed when the phone
rang, waking me up so instantly that I felt a slight
pain in my head. With an unsteady hand, I picked the
receiver up. 'Hello. Is he all right?' I asked without
even waiting to find out who was on the other end of
the phone.

'Who?' a puzzled voice asked. It sounded
unfamiliar. It wasn't that of Dr. Okon. I felt
disappointed and ashamed of myself. 'I'm sorry, but
who is speaking?' I asked. He told me his name and

asked if he could speak to Dr. Okon. I replied that Dr. Okon was not in the house but asked if I could take down the message.

He told me that a member of his family was sick and so needed the doctor's attention. I assured him that I would deliver the message. He replaced his receiver. For a long moment I went on holding my own receiver to my ear. I felt like holding on to it. Why should this man disturb me at this hour of the night, I asked myself crossly. I decided to go down to the hospital and see how Baba was doing. It was an impossible idea. I couldn't possibly walk to the hospital at this time of the night and no taxi would be plying the road outside. I made my way slowly to the settee and began to doze once again. The telephone rang. It came from the hospital; it was his voice. 'Hello, is that Onyemowo?' 'Yes, speaking... has he survived? Were you able to save his life?' I asked, not waiting to hear from him. 'Baba died.'

'What! How... Why... died?' I burst into tears. I could not bear to talk any longer. I dropped the receiver down on the table and ran weeping back to my room.

Chapter 9

In two weeks' time, it would be Christmas. People had already started doing some shopping for the seasonal celebrations. Parents could be seen at every entrance and corner of the supermarkets in the town, dragging their children along with them. The road traffic was getting heavier with every day that passed. I did not join in the preparations. I did not need to buy much for the baby; I had other plans for her at Christmas.

All I had to get for myself was a new dress. If Dr. Okon had not pressured me into buying a new dress for that day, I doubt if I would have bothered. Three days earlier, an invitation had arrived, addressed to 'Dr. and Mrs. Okon,' inviting us to attend a grand party for all the doctors working in the Murtala Mohammed Hospital. This party was planned for the 25th of December, which was Christmas Day. It was to be held at the Minister of Health's residence.

Dr. Okon showed the card to me the very day he received it. 'You'll need a really nice new dress for this,' he said. 'I don't have the money for a dress,' I lied. I did have enough money for the dress, but the fact was that I did not want to spend it. For some time now, I have been saving a good portion of my earnings. I needed the money for a new start after Idu came back home—if ever we got together again. Because of this, I had taken to asking the doctor for almost everything I wanted to buy. 'I will give you the money. No trouble about that. Is that all right?' he assured me.

So far I had not bought the dress. On several occasions, he had asked me whether I had got the dress or not, and as many times I had told him that there was still enough time for any Christmas purchases. And this might be the last shopping I ever did in this house, I told myself. As I turned over on my side to face Dr. Okon, who lay beside me, the pillow that supported my head rolled over and fell on the floor. He pushed his heavy arm under my head and, gently, I made my head comfortable on it. It was early Friday morning. I did not know exactly what time it was, for I felt too sleepy to get out of bed and go to the table on which my wristwatch lay. But I think the time was about five-thirty. There was still plenty of time before we had to get up. We relied on Naomi to warm up the water for our baths. She used to wake up as early as six to prepare our breakfast. Nobody ever needed to wake her up. She always woke up before six.

Dr. Okon was already wide awake. He cuddled me under the thick cloth that covered us both. 'Onyemowo,' he called my attention. 'Yes,' I answered. 'I will be traveling to your village tomorrow.' 'To do what?' 'I want to see your people.' 'About what?' He held me tighter. I felt protected by his presence, but I felt more protected when I was with Idu. 'I want them to change their minds.'

'They can't change their minds over me. I have gone against our customs. Nobody can do that without paying the price. It is a waste of time going to see them.' 'I'm going to find out the truth about it.' 'Are you accusing me of being a liar then?' 'No. But I want to verify the facts.' He stood his ground. 'And who do you think my people are?' I asked. 'Your parents, of course.' 'But I told you they are no more.' He observed a minute of silence for the dead and apologized for his mistake. 'Then I will inquire after your relatives in the village.' 'Do you know my village?'

'I will find it. You once told me that you came from Upu village in Otukpo, Benue State. When I get there, I will surely find somebody who will direct me to your relatives.' 'But I no longer belong to the village. Nobody knows me there. Nobody cares to know...'

'Even if nobody knows you there in the village, the villagers know your father and his relatives. His relatives will know about you. So I foresee no trouble about tracing your people at all,' he assured me. Early that morning, Dr. Okon left for my state, for my town, for my village, for my clan and even for my relations. I wondered what he would tell them. Would he inform them that he had put me in the family way and would like to marry me? And would they approve the marriage? My parents were still alive and perfectly healthy. But I had lied to him that they were no more, and he had believed it, I thought.

When Idu had been involved in the motorcycle accident, I had written to them telling them what had happened. Then when he had been transported overseas for treatment like a commercial packet, I had written to them again to inform them about his leaving. They understood how I felt about the incident and had sympathized but advised me to exercise patience until his return. But since I had become pregnant, I had never gone home or even written again, because I could not bear the shame of being made pregnant by any man other than my fiancé. If they should tell Dr. Okon the truth about our marriage customs then things would surely prove hard for me.

That very week my junior brother came to the house, making it the most confusing time of my life and almost leading me to fight against my will. He had just gained an admission into the School of Basic Studies in the North. Immediately his admission letter had arrived, he had written telling me about his success. I had written back congratulating him and saying that now that the Benue State Scholarship was an automatic process there would not be any problem about him studying in the institution. But I had never once paused to think of the word 'automatic' as applied to the English vocabulary of the people of the state, at least not until now. When my junior brother, Ochiefe, came he was in red and I could hardly guess what was in the air.

Ochiefe was the only one in the family to whom I entrusted my confidence. He was fat, energetic and dark in complexion and did not resemble any of us in character, for he was like the wind, changing from time to time. Even his build was very different from anyone else's. Our father often teased that our mother must have cheated him by bringing Ochiefe into the family. Ochiefe was the only one who knew about my plan for my fiancé, Idu. Once or twice I had thought of telling him of my intentions for the baby, but I changed my mind about it at the last minute, fearing that his reactions might be contradictory to mine, and possibly dangerous to the plan.

Dr. Okon was still absent from home. He was not yet back from trying to find my people. Ochiefe had arrived from Makurdi hoping to talk to him about various problems but, seeing that Dr. Okon was not in the house, he wondered whether he ought not to go back to the village and meet him there. I, however, pressed him to stay a day or two before leaving. In fact, he had a real problem with the scholarship board in the state. As he described his experiences at the scholarship office when he had gone there to negotiate for his scholarship, it seemed certain that he had suffered greatly. After the evening meal, we both took our seats in the parlor. The little baby was on my lap. Ochiefe was nearly in tears.

'I need help from both of you. Without it my studies in this institution will not be possible. I'm really in need of help, especially from your husband,' he said slowly. 'I'm getting desperate.' 'What sort of help is that?' I asked. 'Sponsorship.' 'What about the automatic scholarship from the state?' 'They are not ready to give it to me.' 'Why? Isn't the award automatic? How can they deny you the state scholarship when you have a right to it?' I asked anxiously.

At first, I had thought he was trying to make a joke out of everything, but now I began to realize how serious the problem was. My baby coughed and brought up some of her meal. I wiped her mouth with a white handkerchief that I kept especially for that sort of thing. 'I quarreled with the man at the top,' he said, running his hand over the bushy hair on his head. 'Why on earth did you have to quarrel with them? You know very well that your education depends on them. We come from a poor family and you know it. Why do you have to fight the man at the top? Tell me, for goodness sake, why...?'

'I did not fight him, for God's sake! I only told him what I felt about him. That shouldn't stop him from giving me my share of the money, should it?' 'No, it shouldn't, but you must realize that you cannot just express your personal feelings about the top officials of the government. You just have to keep a quiet lip about certain things because you are poor.'

'We are not all poor. After all, your husband is a medical doctor. He is a rich man. He can help...'

'Help in what way...?' I interrupted. I was so anxious to know what he had said to the man at the scholarship office that I returned to the first subject. 'What exactly did you tell that man, Ochiefe?' 'I didn't tell him much. I was not allowed to do so,' he said, then paused to think. 'You know that I was late in applying for admission into the institution? Immediately the place was offered to me, I went down to the scholarship board offices with the intention of getting the state scholarship to study for my course. When I got there, I asked them about the scholarship form I had earlier sent my money for, pointing out that I had never received it. But nobody was prepared to listen to me. Because I could not get the one I had sent my money for, I decided to buy a new one in place of the lost one, so I went into the office of one of the top men who was interviewing the students seeking the award and asked for a new form. He, however, seemed totally unconcerned, maintaining that all the application forms had already been processed and that I should call back in two days' time. Two days later, I went back to see the same fat old man. Do you know he's got tribal marks that make his face look permanently miserable! I

84

asked him about the form. This time he refused even to listen to me and ordered me to go away. I was so angry that right there, in front of the students, I told him what I thought of him.'

'Come on, you haven't answered my question yet. What did you actually say to him?' I was determined to know all the details.

'Among other things, I pointed out to him that he had diverted the money that I had sent for the form into his own private use. Then I told him that it would be his fault if I didn't get the state scholarship.' 'How certain are you that he was the actual person who received the money? How do you know whether the money for the form did reach his office? How can you be sure that the Post Office is not involved in this business?' I asked him. 'But... all right, what about the new form I asked him to get for me?' 'He told you they were not available.' 'He never told me that; he just yelled at me to get out of his office.' 'But you told me that was what he said!' 'That was on the first day I went there.'

'Well, I think he sent you out like a dog because of the way you approached him in his office. You must realize that everybody likes to be treated with respect in his own office, even an office messenger.'

Outside the house, I could hear that the wind was blowing strongly. I thought for a few moments then slowly asked, 'Don't you know anybody else there who could help you out with the form?' 'I told you, nobody is ready to help me there.' 'Try again. This time you might succeed.' 'I'm not going back to that office.''Then I will go and fight it out for you.' 'Don't go there, Onyemowo. I warn you, don't go there for my sake.' 'Then what do you want to do now?' 'Your husband may be able to help with the sponsorship,' he said, with confidence.

It baffled me to see my brother like this. Had he forgotten so quickly about what I had told him? Did he think that I was now legally married to Dr. Okon and had at last forgotten about Idu? It made my blood run cold to hear him refer to Dr. Okon as my husband. Unfortunately or fortunately, Dr. Okon did not have enough money for such a big project. Even if he had, would he have used it for my brother? I burst out, 'What are you talking about, Ochiefe? Do you really know exactly what you are asking?' He brushed down his goat-like beard, smiled at me and said, 'I know your problems. But you just have to understand something. Now listen to me carefully and...'

'What do you want me to understand?' I interrupted. 'You understand nothing yourself. Do you, Ochiefe, even think about my problems? Do you understand the agonies I have been undergoing all these months? I really believe that you can't be bothered to understand and none of my people understand either.' I burst into tears.

My brother was sympathetic—he had always been fond of me. He spoke to me, softly, in a comforting voice. With his back resting against the cushioned chair, he told me he would no longer try to further his education if that was conflicting with my wishes. He would rather remain jobless, without further education, even if it meant him joining up with the gangs of armed robbers in another big city, rather than go back to the scholarship board.

I felt pity for him and found myself asking him blindly, 'Tell me, what do you want me to do for you?' 'It is nothing. Forget about it,' he said, standing up and adjusting the position of the socks on his feet. 'Sit down and let us discuss everything like a brother and sister before Dr. Okon comes back home,' I said. He moved closer to me and took the tiny little fingers of my baby in his and teased her, 'Pretty lady.' I pulled him down to sit beside me.

'I apologize if I annoyed you,' he said. 'As you can see, I'm in a fix. I want you to marry the doctor. I know he loves you dearly and he will do everything just to keep you as his wife and make you happy. And this is the contract we are going to make.' He paused. 'We shall join our hands and drain his pocket after the two of you have become a wife and a husband. This contract will last only a few years. And after that, you may dissolve the marriage. It is possible that you can ...'

My head felt dizzy, and I wondered if I was going to collapse on the carpet. I no longer could hear what my brother was saying. None of what he was telling me made any sense. I wanted to shout at him to stop it, but I felt as if my tongue was fastened on to my palate. I could not utter a word and I felt like crying like a little girl.

'Idu is not the only man on this earth who would make a good husband. There are many other ones who would prove better husbands than your fiancé, Idu. Anyway he... he is already crippled... I mean, you should think it over, Onyemowo. What is wrong with Dr. Okon being your husband, anyway? He is a medical doctor. What better' husband do you ... ?'

I shouted at him to stop. I could not bear to hear any more. I could not imagine myself sacrificing my life for two people. I had done it for Idu and now, here was my brother demanding the same thing from me for him.

Ochiefe got up and left the room in a hurry. I could not figure out exactly what he had said just before stepping out of the parlor, but I think it was something about leaving town and that I would see him no more. There, in the spacious parlor, I was left alone with my baby on my lap.

Chapter 10

It was the 16th of December. Idu, my fiancé, was due back home on the 30th. If I wanted to do anything before his homecoming, it would have to be between now and the 26th. Dr. Okon had just arrived back from my hometown, and Ochiefe had left the day before for no definite destination. He had left without waiting to see the doctor. I could see that something had brought about a change in the life of the father of my baby as soon as he emerged from his little car outside the house with his briefcase. As he got out, closing the door behind him, he did what he had not done for many months now. As I stood at the door of the house, ready to welcome him back home, he walked straight to where I stood, his black briefcase in his hand and his brown jacket hanging over his right arm, smiling. He came up to me, hugged me, and gave me a big kiss on my lips. I did not rebuff the sign of affection he showed to me. In fact, I felt good to be receiving that kiss from him. As we parted, the doctor sighed.

'My darling... My little bird,' he said, putting the jacket over my shoulders and looking at me lingeringly. 'You look so beautiful this evening. Smile at me and let me see more of your beauties; the beauty of a girl is incomplete without a warm smile showing on her lips. So, smile at me, and let me feel good this evening.' He was smiling. I did as he asked me to. 'Yes, that is better. I feel so happy now. How is the baby?' he asked. 'Fine,' I answered, leading the way to the parlor. We went past the parlor to his room where I put the jacket down in a corner, ready to go to be drycleaned the next day. 'How was the journey?' I asked.

'The journey was a marvelous one. It was the most successful journey I have ever made in my life. Where is the baby?' 'She is with Naomi at the back of the house.' 'Is Naomi better?' 'Yes, she seems to have recovered,' I answered. He left the room and, going back to the door, he raised his voice to call Naomi. I went to the kitchen to prepare some food for him. I did not want Naomi to do it for me this evening.

As I bent down with the knife in my hand, peeling off the bark of a yam, I thought of the change in Dr. Okon's behavior that evening. I could not really think of a reason for it. When he had left home to go to Otukpo, he had said he was going to see my parents and then come back to Kano a short time later. When he had come back that evening, he had maintained that the journey had been a marvelous one. Has he seen my people? I could not just tell. I was in the midst of this confusion when he came unannounced into the kitchen with the baby in his arms. He came straight over to me and patted me on the shoulders.

'What a lovely woman I have!' he smiled. He bent down and took a closer look at the yam. 'This is my favorite food. I know you will cook it for me to perfection after my long and tiring journey back here. But why don't you allow Naomi to give you a helping hand?' He looked at Naomi, who was right beside me, scornfully.

'No, it's all right. I told her I would do it specially for you. After all, too many hands spoil the soup,' I said, and looked straight into his eyes with a falsely smiling face. 'Naomi, you may go and look after the car. See that it is clean again after that long journey to our hometown and back to Kano,' I ordered the girl out of the door. She left with her small buttocks bouncing provocatively.

After Naomi had left the kitchen, Dr. Okon placed the baby across his shoulders and started to rock her gently. He took his gaze from the little baby and fixed it on me. 'I found your people after a long search in the town and in the village. Your mother said I should say "hello" to you and the baby...'

'My mother!' I exclaimed, because I had never expected him to find my mother. Before he had left Kano I had told him that my parents were no more. Yet here he stood, delivering a message of greetings from my mother. 'Yes, your mother, and your father as well.' 'Incredible! Incredible!'

'But I told you I had no parents. The people you met in my village must have falsely claimed to be my parents for reasons best known to themselves; they are not my parents in any real sense,' I told him.

'We shall discuss it later," he said and left the kitchen with the baby on his shoulders. At the hour when the moon was just beginning to climb over the rim of the horizon in the east, Dr. Okon and I brought two armchairs out of the house. I had already put on my nightgown. Tonight, the weather was a bit of an improvement on the previous week, though it was the month of December. A sudden light breeze lifted the light garment I was wearing, exposing the skin of my thighs. I covered them up. Dr. Okon was also in black pajamas which he had bought two weeks ago. He had earlier complained of back-ache and said that he would not go outside the house tonight but would remain indoors after his long and exhausting journey.

However, there we both sat, facing each other with a small table separating us on which two identical bottles of coca-cola lay open. To my left was the garden to which the old man, Baba, had dedicated himself and in which he had met his death.

Dr. Okon raised up his eye-glasses and spoke about the journey that had taken him out of Kano for three days. There, in the moonlight, he narrated to me how, in trying to locate where my people lived, he had suffered greatly. At last, he said, he had found them and had asked them about the marriage customs among the Idoma people as regards a baby born into the family before the actual marriage. They had told him a story quite contrary to the one I had told him just before he left. He concluded by saying, 'Through an interpreter, I disclosed to your parents that I was the very man who had put you in the family way and that I was a doctor. After they had welcomed me and water had been brought to me to quench my thirst, they asked about you and the baby. I told them what had brought me to them all the way from Kano. They held counsel among themselves and later gave me this answer, which was interpreted for me in English.

"We shall not give our daughter to a stranger to marry."'

I could no longer hold my temper in check, and so I cut his story short. 'Tell me what was the last thing that happened between you and my people.' He lowered his voice and spoke very coolly. 'Onyemowo, you know how much I love you. I sometimes wonder what is happening to me when it comes to my love for you. Despite your low educational qualifications, as compared with mine, I still love you and would like to maintain you as a good wife. I have tried many times to get some satisfaction from other girls, but I have never once succeeded in doing so. And due to this constant failure I...'

'Do you mean to tell me that you do not get more satisfaction from that girl of yours, Ruth, than you do from me? And are you now trying to say that you have decided to use me as a last resort, after everything else has failed?' I cut in.

'Come now, Onyemowo. Ruth is not my wife. I have only been to her once and failed to get any satisfaction out of her, so I have given her up. This is what you must try to understand. A girlfriend is a girlfriend, and a wife is a wife. Can't you see the distinction between the two?' he asked with a laugh.

'And that explains why you ignore me sometimes? You do so because I'm not your wife?' 'But you are now.' 'Pardon?' 'I mean that you are now my wife and so you will henceforth be treated as a wife... I have paid the bride-price to your people. You are now mine,' he said, then paused. 'Tomorrow, we shall write to Idu Idoko and congratulate him on his wedding plans with the white lady he mentioned in the letter he wrote to you. We shall also tell him about our marriage. After the Christmas celebrations, we shall all go down to my hometown and see my people. My people need to know about our marriage—it is necessary that they know about it, I think.' 'How much money did you give them as the bride-price, if I may ask?' 'One thousand naira,' he said flatly.

My head felt heavy on my neck when I heard the huge amount of the money that had been spent in order to sell me to the one I did not love. He was twice as old as I was. I just could not love him. I tried to keep my temper while he spoke about his contract with my people, my parents. And so I told him that it was a good amount of money he had paid to my parents, despite the government's decision to peg down the bride-price in the State to the barest minimum, which was far lower than that amount.

Sitting there before him, I was like a goat taken to the market and sold to any man who wants her at a price and against her own will. My parents were now acting against my will. They should at least have consulted me before taking this action. But they had failed to do so, which was very bad of them. At least, I thought, I was old enough to decide on my own. I thought of going to see them at Otukpo to ask them why they had taken this rash decision. They wouldn't have done such a thing in normal circumstances. Something critical must have happened at home which had compelled them to do so, I thought. I gulped down a mouthful of coca-cola, placed the bottle back on the table, looked at the doctor and said, 'I want to go home, Doctor."When?' he asked.

'Tomorrow.'

'To do what?'

'I just want to go home. I want to see my people about marriage matters...' 'What about marriage matters? Is anything wrong with the marriage?' he asked, relaxing back against the light armchair. 'Are you not happy that we are now married?'

'I'm happy we are married. That is why I'm going home tomorrow. I must go and perform some of the necessary rites before I settle down fully here with you...'

'These rites again!' he cried out. 'You once told me lies concerning the marriage customs in your area and now you are telling me about rites, rites, rites! How many? How do I know if this is not another of your bunch of pretty lies? You are not going.'

'Why?'

'Because it is not necessary for you to go.' 'Then I will go against your will.' 'You will not go as long as I live and as long as you remain with me as my wife.' I couldn't believe my ears. In a matter of three days everything was over and I had now become a wife to an aging man with less than the full amount of hair on his head. There he sat, boasting of married life. Why, why should I, Onyemowo, be expected to boast of the same thing? 'Are you trying to say that the amount you paid to my people has bought me, has made me a wife to you? And if that is what you are thinking, then I must prove to you that you are totally wrong in your calculations. What you fail to understand is that you have not finished doing those things that are necessary to make a man a husband.'

'What else remains to be done? As far as I'm concerned, there is nothing more to be done in order to make you my wife. The court in your town has already proved its efficiency by approving the marriage between me and you. Your parents have also signed the contract. Nothing was left undone before I left the area, I'm certain.'

He must be joking! How could the court approve of a 'till death us do part' marriage without the consent of the bride who is the core of a successful marriage? Then I thought of asking him how that could be possible. He must have been duped by a group of the villagers from my area. How could an educated man like Dr. Okon be duped in the daytime by a group of illiterate villagers who must have claimed to be my parents! And were they really my parents? I tried to explain everything to him and got the surprising reply from him that with him everything within the country was possible. He told me that I need not worry about his being duped.

I did not agree with him, but I pretended that I did. Had he not worked a miracle barely a year ago? Had many people not been struck with amazement at how he had been able to convince the Kano State Ministry of Health both to send Idu Idoko abroad for treatment and to pay the bill? Why then did I doubt his ability to force my parents to sign the contract without me being present in the court?

With a final word from him that I was now under his full control and that I could do nothing without his approval, he got up from his seat and went into his room. I presumed he was going to get dressed and leave the house until later that night. As he was on his way through the parlor, I called out to him and told him about my brother's coming in his absence. 'I hope nothing serious has happened to him,' he said, turning round. 'No. Nothing serious... nothing much, really,' I stammered.

'What do you mean by nothing much?' he asked sharply. I realized that he was rather concerned about my brother's coming.

'What I mean is that he did not come for any specific purpose. He only came to say hello to us and go back,' I lied. He removed his eye-glasses and bent down to scratch his right leg. 'But none of your people has ever come to this house. That is why I'm...' 'And that is because none of them knows where...' 'Why didn't he wait to see me before he left?'

'He waited... but... It was about the state scholarship. He had a quarrel with the top officials at the ministry and he is afraid of going back to them. He left here in a bad frame of mind. I fear what will happen to him.' 'Do you mean about his scholarship?'

'No. Not only about that. He said he would join up with a gang of armed robbers, probably in Lagos, instead of going back to the scholarship board.' 'A gang of armed robbers?' he asked nervously.

'Exactly that. And he means to do exactly what he said he would do. I understand his way of thinking. The lives of those top officials are in danger if he should be let loose.' 'But money has never been a part of our problems. We can sponsor him to further his education. Why didn't you stop him from taking such an evil decision?' He paused. 'Is there any way you think it might be possible for us to stop him from doing such a thing before he gets caught up in that business and spoils our good name, Onyemowo?'

'Not unless I can go and bring him back so that you can talk sense into him about the evils behind the business and also about the sponsorship,' I suggested.

He did not say a word; he just turned on his heel and went to his room. I thought I was playing a good trick on him. I thought that when I suggested this idea clearly to him, he would allow me to go home the next day. I never had it in my mind that he would see through the depth of my tricks and ruin my plan. Early the next morning, I left for my home town under the pretext of going after my brother. It was a tough game leaving Dr. Okon and the family of two—my daughter and Naomi. The baby could now boast of a name, after the many arguments over the best name for her. After many battles, I had decided that she should be called Eno. In fact, the name was suggested by her father and approved by me. It was the name of his grandmother, so he said. I believed him because I did not know his grandmother. I never even wondered whether any of his own people bore that name or not. I believed him implicitly. I had to believe him. Very soon, I thought, that name and the owner of the name would go back to the very dust from where they had come. The naming ceremony had not been a great success. Dr. Okon had drunk too much wine and had become argumentative. He had had a lot of apologizing to do the next day. It did not augur well for little Eno.

When I got home, my father told me all that had happened on the arrival of Dr. Okon. He told me that they had done what they were asked to do in order to save a situation which was not far from landing them in jail. My mother, when she saw me coming from afar, could not face me with those guilt-stricken eyes. But my father stood to face me. He had often said in the past that a man does not run away from danger. That was why he felt bold enough to tell me what had happened at home while I was away in Kano.

It all happened because of my older sister. She had for many years been living happily with her husband, but suddenly things took a different shape. She and her husband had had a little misunderstanding, and she left him to go to an unknown place, leaving her four children behind. Until this time, nobody had heard anything about her, or her whereabouts. Then, suddenly, the whole trouble burst out. The husband demanded his wife, my sister, from my father. But the old man could not produce her. Then the husband demanded his dowry back in lieu of his wife. My father had no money and no way of getting any. Ochiefe was not able to give any help. He had, right from childhood, sworn that he would never pay a kobo as compensation over any of his sisters who might venture to leave her husband. So nobody expected anything of him.

My father went on to say that it was at this point, just before the matter had come to court, that Dr. Okon had come to him and asked to marry me. To my parents, Dr. Okon had appeared like a Messiah. So they had collected the money from him for my bride-price and paid back the dowry of my sister, who was nowhere to be found. Only God knew exactly what had happened to her, and only God knew when she would come back home.

As my father went from one part of the tale to the other, he had difficulty in preventing a flood of tears pouring from his red eyes. If it had been my mother the flood of tears would have swallowed up her eyeballs. There was nothing more I could say. Nothing. Nothing... Absolutely nothing I could say to my parents about what had happened. I knew they would understand how I felt about it.

I had to talk to my brother Ochiefe concerning his education and his wrong decision to join up with the armed robbers that was sure one day to lead him to the post where he would be fired at by authorized armed men. I must talk to him about Dr. Okon's willingness to help him further his education. I could well imagine how happy he would feel after hearing the news.

But sadly, the news was that he had left home a day before my arrival. Nobody could tell me exactly where he had gone. That very day, I went back to Kano with a heavy heart. My brother had gone! I had to go back to Eno and her father, Dr. Okon, against my will.

Chapter 11

Christmas was almost upon us. As I boarded the taxi cab to go to Sabon Gari market to do some shopping for the coming of the great day, I thought of Idu and what I must do before his coming back to the country. And as I finally got out of the taxi with a hand outstretched to hand over the fare to the taxi driver, I thought of how my sister's plight had landed me in this muddle. Now I must remain a housewife to Dr. Okon against my wishes. Whether I liked it or not, he was now my legal husband. I needed to see my sister and talk to her about it. But how and where could I see her? She had left her husband's home without informing anybody of where she was going, and she had not written to anyone since she had left home.

I crossed over to the other side of the busy road. Despite the fact that it was still the early hours of the morning, when all the working-class men and women were still at work, the market was already crowded with people. I was no longer a worker. My husband had decided to stop me from working. He maintained that the money he was earning was enough for the whole family and so it was not necessary for me to work. I had tried to insist on working, but he had forced me to give up the job. I had a feeling that things would not be as easy for me if I had to stay at home all the time. There are a good number of things a wife should not have to keep on demanding from her husband, so if she keeps on working life is much easier and more worth living. Later, however, I discovered that things would not be as hard for me as I expected. This was because there was a constant reserve of money at home for me to draw on—more than enough for my wants with some left over to send home to my parents. Dr. Okon had his own practice, a private practice elsewhere, nothing to do with the Ministry. From this source, the money kept on flowing to the family.

From shop to shop, people kept on struggling to make their way through the crowds. With only five days to go until Christmas, I was still unsure about what would actually happen on the day of the celebration. So I continued with the shopping, hoping I was doing the right things. I could have bought everything I really needed from any of the 'hench' supermarkets if Dr. Okon had not insisted that I should buy things like rice from the 'common' market. This was nothing to do with the low cost of it in the Sabon Gari market, he maintained. The fact was that the rice in the Sabon Gari market contained much more carbohydrate than that of the supermarkets, called polished rice. Because of his theories about polished and unpolished rice, I did as he wanted and bought the family rice in the Sabon Gari market. This morning I was there again.

As I bent down to bargain for a mudu of the white rice, the price of which had recently soared, I felt a light touch at the base of my neck. At first I thought it was one of those load-carriers who were struggling to get into the shop I was buying from, so I did not respond to the touch.

Onyemowo,' somebody called. It was a female voice and I thought it was a very familiar one. I turned my head to take a good look at the owner of the voice. Oh, what a marvelous sight! I just couldn't believe my eyes when I saw my sister, my senior sister, standing right behind me. I immediately placed the mudu of rice I had in my hand on the ground and grabbed her hand. Then I thought that was not enough of an embrace, so I hugged her fat body. A good number of the fast-moving people— the market men and women—stopped to take a look at us.

'Is it really you?' I spoke for the first time, almost too excited to articulate properly. 'Is it really you, Onyemowo?' she asked. 'I thought I would never see you again.' 'Why should you think that?' 'I thought maybe I didn't want to see you again. I saw you the moment you stepped into the market and, as you were coming this way, I dodged you. But then I realized that I was only fooling myself by running away from you and that we would surely meet one day as long as we are both living in this town, we are bound to see each other...' 'Where have you been?'

'It is a long story... But at last I'm here in this town,' she replied. 'Doing what?' I asked, studying her closely. She had really grown fat. 'Nothing,' she answered shortly. 'Nothing? You mean you are here doing nothing?' 'What I mean is that I'm now a free woman.' I considered her answer. 'So, my sister has become a woman of the hotels since leaving her husband.' I said slowly, 'I see...' There was not much more to say. 'After you have finished your shopping, I will take you to where I'm lodging at the moment. We can talk more freely there. At any rate, hurry up and get what you have to buy, then we can go.'

It was getting on towards noon. After buying all the necessary things, we walked together out of the busy market and took a taxi to the International

Hotel, where my senior sister was lodging. As the taxi drove us through the streets, I kept on stretching forward to look at my sister who sat in the front seat, beside the driver. I could not believe my eyes; I just couldn't believe that she was not a ghost. How had she managed to remain in the town for the past year without anybody coming across her? I began to tell her about my life.

The taxi turned its nose and pulled up at the hotel. We stepped out and she paid the man the fare from the market to the hotel. My sister lived upstairs. Shoulder to shoulder, we climbed the steep stairs to her room. Above the door of her room was written, ROOM 6. She did not live there alone. A woman of the same profession shared the room with her. The two of them had to share the small apartment in order to pay the bills. In this way, the burden of the rent was made lighter for each of them. Though the room was very small, it contained two beds. A curtain separated the one from the other.

The room smelled of yesterday's soup. They must have been using it as a kitchen as well as a sleeping place. To my left was a cooking stove with a new, full pot of soup on the top. This proved that they had been cooking indoors. My sister carefully placed her shopping on the floor beside the stove.

She then pulled back the blue curtain by one of the beds and asked me to take a seat on it. She took the bag containing all I had bought from the market from me and I sat down on the eight-spring bed.

'My neighbor... Neighbor... You dey sleep? Look, my sister don come O,' my sister called loudly. A voice answered from inside the curtain opposite my sister's bed. From the trembling curtain I knew somebody was inside there. As well as the feminine voice, I could hear a low voice that much resembled that of a large man.

'My neighbor, my sister just dey come O,' my sister said again. 'True? Welcome, sister,' the other said without much interest. The bed opposite creaked. My sister turned her attention to me with a smiling face and said, 'That is my neighbor who is talking from behind the curtain. She is an Ibo. All the prostitutes lodging here are Ibos. I'm the only one who comes from a different tribe. In fact, all of them are very good to me. I enjoy staying with them. They treat me like their sister. Very soon they will pour in, one after the other, if they discover that you are here. Now, you must be very hungry. You need some food to keep you alive, I think?' She patted my back and commented on my slimness saying that I could not be feeding properly. I was pleased, and pretended to be flattered. She laughed and went towards the standing stove.

'I'm not feeling very hungry,' I told her. 'But I can see the signs of hunger on your face. Your stomach looks very flat and resembles that of a tortoise. I know you are hungry,' she said. 'Oh, yes, yes. I understand. I know you do not want to eat food in the house of harlots. You are...' 'I eat anywhere, anytime and with anybody when I'm hungry. I do not mind the conditions of this place and I do not notice the conditions of any place where I eat, either. Is a harlot not a human being? Are you not my sister? Should I reject your food on the grounds that you are a harlot? I know it is the bad conditions of your life that have brought you to this place. You were not born to be here or to be a harlot. Anyway, I am sure that you people here eat much better food than we do. The fact that I'm the wife of a doctor does not mean that my living conditions are better than yours. The fact is that I'm not hungry,' I asserted.

'That is all right, then. Now what do you want to drink?' 'Nothing, thank you,' I answered. 'Your way of life is really different from ours. You will neither take food nor drink beer in my house. You do not belong to us. It is hard being a harlot, my sister.' 'I know it is hard. But how did you come to be here and why is it that none of our people has ever managed to discover your whereabouts?' I asked her.

She left the cooking stove, came back and sat with me on the bed. She placed her hands gently on the bed behind her and leaned her heavy body on them, completely relaxed. I hardly ever leave the hotel during the daytime. I don't want anybody to discover that I'm here,' she said. 'It might spoil things.' 'But today you felt bold enough to go to the market where our people might well be part of the crowd. Don't you think you could have been spotted?' 'Today... I just don't know what took me out of this place to the market...' 'Are you saying that today was the first day you have been to the market since you came into this hotel?' She nodded thoughtfully. 'Why did you leave your husband?' I asked. 'He is an irresponsible man.'

'In what way?'

A woman with a fat body, fatter than my sister, poked her nose into the room. She greeted my sister, and asked her if she had a visitor from home. My sister told her that I was her junior sister and wife to a doctor, emphasizing the title, DOCTOR. The woman stood apparently rooted to the spot without saying another word. From her look I could gather that she was surprised to face one of my sister's relatives. Then she smiled and walked towards me to welcome me. After this, she went out of the room to tell all other neighbors that a sister of their 'neighbor' had come.

As I watched her leaving, I wondered whether all the other women lodging there in that hotel had fat bodies. My sister was fat and this woman was very fat; perhaps they were all fat. Bit by bit, the room began to fill with the female lodgers—all of them prostitutes, as I gathered later from my sister. Before them, I appeared as a head of state receiving a grand welcome from her subjects. Then, in a twinkle of an eye, the room became filled up with alcoholic drinks. The noise echoed and re-echoed. It was now getting to three in the afternoon. At last I began to feel that the festivities were beginning to do me more harm than good. I felt that what little time I had should have been employed in talking to my sister. So, as everyone else drank, I asked my sister to tell me everything that had happened since she had left her husband to join up with this group of prostitutes. I also asked, 'Why did you say your husband was not a responsible man?'

'My husband, as everybody knows, was a good man,' she said. 'But then, his behavior changed. He was no longer what he had been. He hardly slept at home and was often seen with a woman or two. His monthly salary no longer came home to buy food for the children. Every time he came back home after several days outside with the free women, it meant trouble for the whole household. He used to come back drunk and beat up the entire family, including the little ones. Hunger... that was what I could not bear to see my children suffering from.' She took a gulp of her drink and continued, 'Hunger! There is nothing I hate in this world more than hunger. Why should I starve to death while I see other women eating to their fill and throwing a great quantity to the dogs? Because of this, I decided that I should end my suffering by running away from him. Do you have any news about my little children?'

I ignored the question and asked her if she had cleared up the problems with the dowry. I knew she had not yet been informed about the recent payment made through my unwanted marriage with Dr. Okon. I just felt compelled to ask her in order to see her reactions. She replied that she had not done so but was working tooth and nail towards getting enough money to pay off the debt, which might be done in a short time, after the Christmas celebrations perhaps. That would give her the total freedom she had been craving for. I did not want to tell her what had happened in regards to the money collected from Dr. Okon. This information must be reserved until the appropriate time.

'Do you enjoy the work you are now doing in this hotel? Wouldn't you like to leave it and settle down with your children?' I asked her. She shook her head. 'I can't say I like the work. It is hard and disgraceful. Any business that can only be carried out at night and not during the day is a dangerous business. Consider the pain... Horrible things happening in the... It is not a good job, but it is profitable, I assure you. I can't leave it at the moment but I will do so one day. The right time has not yet come for me to do so.'

'But you should come back home and take care of your children who are now suffering. Perhaps you might marry another man who will be able to care for you.' 'I can't come back home, Onyemowo, not now. Where are the children?' 'They are still with their father.' She sighed heavily. The beer continued to be poured out and the women played music on the radio-cassette belonging to my sister's room-mate. They began to dance. The room was now becoming more lively. 'Their father would not leave them with our mother,' I told her. 'Will he ever allow me to see them again?' she was staring into space, leaning back on the bed. 'He ought to.'

One of the women, who had been draining down the beer ever since I had come in, made an excuse and left the room. Another followed her and then another... They were all going to take their daily sleep, as each of them indicated before leaving the room. They had to sleep during the daytime in order to wake up fresh in the evening, ready for the night's business. At last, the room was once again empty of the women who had come to welcome home a sister of their 'neighbor'. Even the man who had been behind the curtain of the bed opposite when I came in was no longer there. He had left earlier with my sister's room-mate, before the room became lively.

My sister and I were alone in the room. It was three-thirty. My husband would by now be wondering where I had gone. I had to go back home in time before he got angry about my absence. But before I went I felt I had to tell my sister all about the dowry problem. So I began, 'I am the one who is now in trouble and not you. I don't think you know that our parents have collected my bride-price from that Calabar man who is now my husband and repaid your husband with the money?' She did not say a word, just listened to me with an open mouth.

'Yes,' I went on, 'they have done so. I did not know about it until he came back to Kano claiming me as a legal wife. I didn't believe him, so, in order to see things with my own eyes, I decided to travel home and ask our parents what happened. It was true that they collected the money from him and paid your husband. You must realize now it never was my wish to marry him properly. But now I'm forced to remain a wife to him as a result of the trouble you had with your husband. Dr. Okon gave our parents one thousand naira and they in turn made use of it to repay your husband...' 'But they shouldn't have done so. Why are they in so much of a haste to repay the man the money?'

'Why shouldn't they be? Your husband threatened to take the matter to the court when you were nowhere to be found. They would have gone to jail if they had failed to repay the dowry money.' 'I just don't know exactly what to say,' she confessed. The confusion showed clearly on her face. Like everybody else who had heard similar news, she looked horrified. 'What... What shall I do now?' 'Go home, of course. Go and see your children. There you can decide on the best thing to do,' I advised. 'I mean about your husband, the Calabar man.' 'Nothing much. But all I know is that I can't stay much longer with him as a wife. I must leave him... Idu is coming back to the country after Christmas.'

'I'm very sorry I have caused all these misfortunes to happen to you at the wrong time. Still, you could decide to divorce him any time when you have enough money and at least there is no baby to worry about...?' 'But I already have a baby girl for him,' I interrupted, almost shedding tears. 'Oh! I didn't know... Well, you need time, don't you. Right now I think we should forget about it. At the moment, I'm free to step out of this place without any fear about what might happen to me. I think perhaps I ought to go with you so that I know where you live in case anything should happen to you there,' she said, trying to ignore my real problems.

I shook my head and asked her not to come to my place yet. Dr. Okon must not know that I had a sister in the town, I told her. 'It is getting late, I must go back home. I will come back and discuss things further with you tomorrow.' 'What about taking food before you leave?' she asked. 'No. Thank you,' I said, getting up.

She went to where my shopping from the market lay and picked it up off the floor. Together, we left the hotel. As a taxi cab stopped close to me, she said goodbye and made me promise to come back the next day. I banged the door of the taxi behind me and told the driver to head for the Nassarawa residential area.

Chapter 12

I watched my baby closely as she played on Naomi's lap. Did she know what my plans for her on Christmas Day were? What a lovely baby Eno was—what a finely shaped mouth she had! What a precious life she would lose! But it was not my fault that Eno should lose that ray of life. It was fate.

It was three days since I had been to see my senior sister at her hotel. When I had left her the other evening, I had promised to return the next day, but I had failed to do so. Tonight, I thought, I must try and go there. Nevertheless, I was aware that my going there might disturb her business if I went during the hours of darkness. Tonight, however, was the best time for me to go to see her. Dr. Okon had gone to Jos and would not be back home until very late in the night. He left after telling me that he was going to see the chief consultant of the General Hospital in Jos. I could not have cared less, even if the purpose of his going there was different from what he had told me. I already knew for sure that in one week our relationship as a husband and wife would be broken.

But what would happen if he came back home before I left the International Hotel? What would be his reaction if he should find me there among the hungry harlots? I knew very well that big trouble would burst out in the house and that I must be shamefully expelled from his life. I had to stay with him even if I were tortured and humiliated by him because of the huge amount of money that bound us together. I must not leave him until the money has been paid back to him in full.

To avoid arousing suspicion over the actions that I intended for Christmas Day, there were a good number of things I had to do in the house before dark. I had to divert every eye from my preparations for carrying out my plan. There was the house to be tidied up. I had to do this with Naomi. While this was going on, I intended to tell her my plan, for it would also involve her. Without her assistance, my plan could not materialize. From now on she would be helping me do everything I wanted to do.

I asked her to come along with a bowl of water and a brush. With the soapy water and the hard brush, we started to scrub the dirty walls. As we worked, we talked. For some time I had been making sure that she found my company very delightful. She had no need to worry about my superiority in the house and over her any longer. I did not want her to feel like a stranger in the family any more, and I knew very well what my reasons were.

'Naomi!' I called. She glanced up at me and I continued, 'It is high time that you had a new dress.' She looked down at herself and examined the tattered dress with a shy smile. 'But I still like it, Madam,' she said. Her reaction surprised me. I had expected her to say, 'Yes, it is old.' What I most liked about Naomi was her intelligence. She had been very quick to learn the standard English spoken in the house. She could now speak like an educated girl, even though she had never been to school in her life. 'Do you really like the dress you are wearing?' I asked her. 'It is still good, Madam,' she repeated. 'Would you like me to get you a new one?' 'I would feel too shy to put it on.' I laughed heartily. 'Are you trying to say that when you put it on, people might laugh at you?' I asked.

'No. They won't laugh at me, but I fear they might stare at me.' 'And what about me? Do people stare at me when they see me in a new dress?' 'They wouldn't do it to you.' I stood with the brush motionless on the wall. 'Why do you say that?' 'Because it is not a strange thing for you to put on a new dress. Apart from anything, nobody would know whether the dress you had on was an old one or not.' 'But they wouldn't know about you either,' I said. 'They would recognize me in this old dress,' she said, examining the material closely. 'Naomi, you are imagining things. Hardly anyone knows about your existence in this town and nobody cares about your movements. So, stop dreaming about silly things like a mad woman. Tomorrow morning I'm going to buy you three different, beautiful dresses. You must wear one of them on Christmas Day. After Christmas, I will buy you some more. Remind me to buy a big box for you so that I can fill it with new dresses.'

Out of excitement, she let the brush she had in her hand fall. 'That can't happen!' she exclaimed. 'It will happen, tomorrow. Tomorrow when you try them on, you will then see yourself as a very beautiful girl standing before the mirror. I will also buy you shoes, a scarf, earrings and necklaces. All these and many other things. I will get them for you tomorrow morning when I go to the market. I will also arrange to have your photograph taken.' 'It is a dream!' 'It is not a dream, it's real.'

'My God! I will go mad about it!' Her voice trembled with excitement. She picked up the brush from the floor and once again we set to work on the dirty wall. As we worked, we discussed the new dresses and how wonderful the coming Christmas would be. Playing in the perambulator beside the standing refrigerator lay Eno, my daughter. 'Naomi,' I called her attention once again. 'Ma,' she answered. 'Do you really want to have new dresses for Christmas Day?' 'Yes. Yes, ma.' 'Well, after I have done all these things for you, would you like to help me and my husband with something?' 'I will do anything you want me to do provided I have the new clothes and as long as people will not laugh at me when I have them on,' she assured me.

As I was about to pour out to her what I had on my mind, my heart began to beat harder and harder within me. Was it Naomi I feared to talk to or was it the effect of what I had to say to her that kept my heart jumping and leaping into my mouth? Was it the lies that I intended to tell as a tactic to bait her that made me afraid? I really could not tell. It is sometimes hard to tell lies in the presence of little children, even a tiny baby.

'Now, this is what I want to tell you. Ever since Eno was born, my husband and I have worried about what might happen to everybody in this house, including you, Naomi.' I paused. 'The baby is a wizard, I promise you...' She stopped working with the brush and took a glance over her left shoulder at the baby lying in the pram.

'She is a witch, I mean,' I continued, 'and we have been trying very hard to take her life before she has the chance to kill all of us in this house. But we are told that because we are her parents, we must not use our hands to kill her and that we must look for another person to do it for us. She would come back to life through birth if either myself or her father should lay a hand on her. For this reason we would be very grateful if you could help in this case. She is a devil.'

Naomi hung her head, meaning that she would not do it or that she feared to do it. 'What do you say about it?' I asked. 'What do you want me to do, Madam?' she asked. 'Kill her! Naomi, kill her!' She shook her head, indicating that the job was too much for her to carry out. 'Kill her!' I repeated. 'Eno is my daughter. Kill her and do everybody a great deal of good. Will you do it, Naomi?' 'No!' 'Why?' 'Because I can't... I just can't do it.'

'I know you would not like to do it under normal circumstances. But you should think of the destruction she will bring on this family if you fail to do it. Then, think of the new dresses I will buy for you. I will also ask the doctor to do a great number of good things for you if you succeed in carrying out what I have asked you to do.'

For a moment, she stood stock still, gazing over my head. Then a large tear rolled down her nose. Another followed and another and... Still, she did not stop gazing at me, neither did she blink. Then she said, 'I will do it.' 'Thank you; you are a good girl. Now you will save the life of everybody in this house. Let me tell you how to go about everything. Tomorrow will be Christmas Day. Dr. Okon and I will be attending an all-doctors' party at the residence of the Minister of Health. We will not take you and the baby along with us. You will all be taken to spend the day with the family of one of our neighboring doctors. It is there that the job will be perfectly done by you.'

She whirled one of her little fingers around her left ear, indicating that she did not fully understand what I was trying to explain to her.

I tried to explain more clearly. 'You and Eno will be taken to spend the day with the children of Dr. Okafor. You will stay there until evening. This is exactly what I want you to do there.' I paused. 'Towards five in the evening, after everybody has settled down in the house, come outside the house with Eno and pretend to be playing with her, out there on the upstairs verandah. Then, for our protection, push her over the railing and let her fall off the three-storey building. Do you understand me, Naomi?' 'I understand, Madam.' 'I will do so.' 'The moment this is done, shout so loudly that everybody in the house can hear that she has fallen.'

'One more thing you must understand,' I continued. 'Never let anybody know about the plan and don't tell my husband about it either. It is not good for you to tell him what I have asked you to do. I will take it upon myself to tell him. He will feel happier if he hears it from my mouth and he will show his gratitude to you by buying you many things as I told you earlier.' 'I won't tell anybody, Madam,' she assured me. 'You are a good girl. 'But the question remained: where would the girl go after she had succeeded in murdering my daughter and after I had left her and Dr. Okon in order to marry Idu? I knew very well that her coming into this house had been for my own sake and she had long been a blessing to me. If I left her now, would she be allowed to remain with Dr. Okon? If she should be asked to quit the house, would she be able to trace her home and her people? If she should stay with the doctor after I had left and the baby had been murdered, was it likely that she would one day reveal to him all that had happened? I was worried that the secret might one day leak out and then spread round the whole town. What would I do if that should happen? I was not sure. One thing was certain, and that was that the police would look for me and get me arrested.

In order not to let her think that the whole idea about the murder of Eno was mine, I decided not to ask her where she would go if she should be asked by Dr. Okon to quit the house. I feared that the doctor would almost certainly insist on it. I sympathized with her and pitied the innocent girl.

Things seemed working out even better than I had expected. We continued to work. As the work continued, I felt that her mind was no longer there with me in the parlor but was concerned with what she had to do on Christmas Day. She must be imagining the first and the last cry of Eno when she landed on her head on the concrete floor below. Was she going to cry at all? I doubted very much that Naomi would cry after the baby had died. I looked over my shoulder, at my daughter lying peacefully in the perambulator and I saw a glimmer of a smile on her face. At about five in the evening of Christmas

Day, would she still be alive to smile? If things worked out according to my plan, her remains would be being gathered up at about that time. No smiling face! But tonight I had to see my sister at the International Hotel.

Chapter 13

As I walked down to the main road to catch a taxi to the International Hotel that dark night, I went over my plan and felt a stab of conscience about Naomi. Oh, poor girl! She had no idea what the aftermath of what I wanted her to do on Christmas Day would be. Even I could not really guess what would happen to her if she really did follow my instructions and commit the murder. Well, she had come into the house in an unexpected manner and so she could disappear in the same way. Where would she go? Had she any real parents to run to if Dr. Okon, in his anger and grief, should threaten to take her dear life after the truth was discovered?

As I reached the two-way road a Beetle car drove past. My heart jumped for I thought it was my husband's. When I realized it was not, I gave out a sigh of relief. How much longer would this fear continue to tear apart the very center of my heart? I wondered. I stood waiting by the roadside for a taxi that would take me to see my sister at the hotel. Ten minutes crept by and still there was no sign of any approaching taxi on the lonely road.

After waiting for thirty minutes without success, I decided to go back home. There was no longer any hope of seeing my sister that night. But I had to see her, it was essential. She needed to be informed about my plans. I needed a helping hand from her and must ask her tonight. It was too far to walk down to her place. Where were all the taxis? There were plenty of private cars and I suppose I could have hitched a lift from any of them. But this might not have been a good idea. It is a basic fact of life that every man who gives a lift to a girl expects to take her to bed. And that was something I had no intention of doing.

Just as I was turning to go, a car went past me and then stopped some yards away from where I stood. As it did so, it blasted its horn, meaning that I should come for a lift. Yes, I knew what the man was after. He must have mistaken me for one of the many prostitutes that hang around the mouth of the Central Hotel ready to be hissed at and picked up in a car driven by any one of the hungry men who drive down that road. I ignored the hooting of the horn and turned up the narrow road that led to our house. Seeing me retreating, he started to reverse his car towards me, trying to catch up with me. Seeing the car moving towards me, I began to wonder if the man inside knew who I was and so was trying to ask where I was going at that hour of the night. What would I tell him if he should ask me the question? I did not know.

Before I had the chance to get off the main road, I was caught up by the car. A handsome face peered out of the driver's window and asked if I needed a lift. I said 'No, thank you,' to him, I was sure that I would soon get a taxi. He explained that I would not get a taxi that night because all the taxi drivers were on strike. He offered to take me wherever I wanted to go. Judging from the smooth way he spoke, I knew he must be one of those womanizers who are ready at all times to do anything within their range to please any female. He had made me an offer and it was now up to me to decide whether to go with him and see my sister tonight or to go back home and miss the chance of talking to her. For a moment I stood undecided. Then I decided to let him give me the lift to the hotel. 'What is your name, if I may ask?' he asked me after a little while. I was ready for that. 'Bella,' I told him. 'That is short for Isabella, I imagine?' 'Exactly.' 'It is a pretty name,' he commented.

'Thank you,' I said. 'And where do you live?' he asked, looking straight at me. 'Right here in Nassarawa.' 'And what do you do for a living?' he went on. I knew why he asked that question. It was because he had just noticed my way of speaking was quite different from that of the free women in the hotels, and he wanted to make sure that he was right.

'I'm a medical doctor,' I released another lie from my bag of distortions. 'I see. But why are you going to that hotel tonight? That hotel is not the sort of place for a decent girl like yourself.'

From his attitude I knew immediately that he had believed everything I said. He also thought that I was too good for him. All the better, I thought. 'There is something very urgent I have to do there. I have just received a telephone call from the hotel manager to say that a member of his staff is dying and asking me to come at once. Actually, the proprietor of the hotel is my relative and I always try to help him if I can.'

We drove on to the hotel. Before I could get out of the car, the man asked me if he could see me the next day. I had already lied to him and said that I was not attached to any man. Not that I cared, I was only interested in getting someone to drive me safely to where I wanted to go and I had succeeded in my wish.

'Why don't we arrange to meet at your house tomorrow?' I suggested. 'Where do you live?' 'At No Man's Land... G.P. 15,' he said.

'Okay, I will meet you there at about four tomorrow,' I lied, then dashed out of the car. 'Thank you for the ride. See you tomorrow afternoon.' I walked into the hotel, and he drove off full of hope that he had caught a new bird. But not me! That type of thing would not happen to me twice, I vowed. Was it not the same sort of car-friendship which had blossomed between me and Dr. Okon last year that was now a thorn in my flesh?

I walked past the tired prostitutes that hung on to their seats waiting for their luck to change. I could guess how they felt. When they heard me they looked up, hoping that another man was coming, each longing for the man to walk straight to them with the raw cash in his hand. But imagine how disappointed they were when they saw me approaching. None of them could recognize me in the dim light that hid their ugly faces from too selective men, so I walked straight upstairs to see my sister, without pausing to look at them. As I hurried past them, I could hear murmurs coming out of their mouths. They no longer welcomed me as their 'neighbor's sister' as they had the day before. The door to her room was locked and it immediately dawned on me that she was probably engaged in another round of 'business'. This was exactly what I had feared might happen. I knew I would be disturbing her in her business tonight, but I just couldn't help it.

Downstairs, I could hear opera music playing. It was chilly waiting there. As I stood in a corner waiting for the door to my sister's room to open, I started imagining what would happen if that man inside with her turned out to be my husband. He would ask me what brought me there so late at night and I, in turn, would tell him straight to his face that I was there to drag him home. That might be very funny, actually. 'What brought you here?' and 'What brought you here?' would be the fight that night. I wondered where her room-mate had gone, for I had not seen her sitting by the door. At last the door opened and a man with a withered leg limped out of the room. Seeing him, I immediately felt sympathetic towards my sister. Imagine having to allow such a deformed man to have anything to do with her.

Onyemowo, so you have come tonight,' my sister said, as I walked in. 'But it is so late... How do you get your husband to allow you to come out at this time of the night when the streets are getting empty of people? How is the baby?' 'My baby is at home,' I told her, 'and my husband has traveled to Jos and may not be back home tonight.' Why did my sister ask so particularly after the baby, my daughter? Did she suspect anything? 'And you seized the opportunity of his being away from home to come out at this hour of the night without fearing the consequences? Just look at how you're dressed, too. You look like a school girl trying to attract the attention of her teacher. I'm sure any man would die for you if he could see you in that sexy dress.'

I smiled, wondering if she was referring to the pair of trousers I had on. 'There's nothing wrong with these, is there?' I asked, pointing at the tight black trousers with the white blouse at the top. 'You do not understand what I'm saying. What I'm trying to tell you is that you should not be trying to attract other men by wearing clothes like that.' 'And what about yours? Are they not attractive?'

'What I wear is a different thing entirely. I have a reason for dressing like this. I have to advertise myself to the men. I'm here for men. And without men, or if my attraction is not felt by men, what is the purpose of my staying here in this hotel? But you,

you are a married woman. Your beauty should not be admired by any other man apart from your husband.'

For a moment, she stood there gazing at the pair of tight trousers. I was beginning to feel very tired. At last she asked me to go inside and take my seat on the only chair in the room. I went in, but refused the seat she had offered me, saying I'd rather sit on the bed. When I was seated she came over and laid her hand on my head. 'What do you want to tell me, Onyemowo?' she asked.

'You already know about it... The awful situation I am in,' I answered. Did she not understand? 'What about my marriage?' she said. 'Do you want to go back to him?' I switched from what I had intended to tell her.

'Stop it, Onyemowo. This is not the time to joke about my marriage! You know as well as I do that I would not go back to that man, that horrible old retired soldier who leaves home every evening with a sober look and comes back home every night drunk. But let me assure you, Onyemowo, if I'm lucky enough to find another man I will marry again. But as I am now, I doubt very much if any man would like to keep me in his house as a wife.' She did not look at me as she smoothed down the hem of her dress. 'But you could still make a good housewife if you wanted to.'

'That is true, Onyemowo. But who will believe that a prostitute can make a good housewife?' she asked. I looked up at her and my eyes caught the mark on her right cheek that made her beauty more colorful, and immediately I knew what hardship in the hands of a stupid husband could do to the beauty of a woman. Right from childhood she had been considered as more beautiful than myself, but now she was not worth a second look.

I could no longer bear to see my sister with bitter eyes or to hear her recounting to me her bitter experiences of marriage. I quickly switched the conversation from her personal problems to mine. 'What I have come to talk about tonight are not your marriage problems but mine... I want to leave my husband,' I said.

'But why should you want to leave your husband, Onyemowo? Is he not an ideal husband for you? Does he not buy you beautiful dresses? Does he not feed you well? Does he not take you to bed as many times as you want him to? Tell me, does he not take care of your baby for you? Or is he coming home every night with another woman and regretting your presence in the house? Answer me; don't just sit there looking at me.' 'It is not a matter of feeding me well or whatever you may think, but...'

She interrupted me fiercely. 'But what? Now tell me, Onyemowo, do you want to become a prostitute just like your sister? I'm not trying to say that nobody would consider marrying an educated girl like yourself if she was a divorcee. But what I'm trying to point out is that men always feel reluctant to marry those girls they consider to be second-hand. If you leave this man, I'm sure you will regret it later. You will find out that things will not work as smoothly as you expected. Because of this, my only advice to you is that you should remain with this man and try to feel contented—even happy with him.'

'But I can't live happily with a man who is old enough to be my father,' I retorted. I saw her face close up when I mentioned his age. I thought perhaps she was at last beginning to see reason and agree with me that it was not all that ideal to remain with him. But I was wrong. 'All I know is that he is doing all he can to make you happy, Onyemowo. You should stay with him and bring up your child. Nowadays, old men can make better husbands than the young men who use their mouths and sweet lips to deceive other girls.'

'Idu wouldn't deceive me,' I said firmly. 'Idu? How do you know he will not deceive you? Apart from that, the boy cannot make a good husband.' 'Why not?' I asked. 'Because he is a cripple,' she said mercilessly. So this was what my people thought of him. They thought he would not come back with his normal health. And my sister agreed with them. Now she was taking me for a fool for falling in love with somebody who might never be able to walk again properly. Not only that—I even hoped to marry him. I had to interrupt quickly to point out that she was wrong about Idu.

'He is not a cripple and that is what you must try to understand. He has completely recovered from the accident and he is coming back home immediately after Christmas.' I moistened my lips. 'But the trouble is that he is coming home with a white girl whom he claims has promised to marry him as soon as he has been discharged from the hospital.'

'Ehe, then, that's the end of that,' she said carelessly. Her statement enraged me so much that I hit the bed with my fist and told her that nothing would ever change my mind about marrying him somehow. 'What plans have you made towards it? Do you think he will really want to marry you after you have disappointed him by having your first baby for another man?' 'My plans will change everything,' I told her.

'What plans?' she asked again. My sister was now beginning to take interest in my problems. I explained to her all I was doing in order to have Idu back as a husband. I even told her about the discussion I had held with Naomi shortly before I left home.

Throughout the revelations of my secrets, my sister did not interrupt me but listened all the while with a keen interest and an open mouth. After I had said the last word to her, she asked, 'Is that what you think best?' I did not answer.

'Onyemowo, have you ever sat down to consider that the baby belongs to you? Don't you ever look back to the pain you experienced during her delivery? How can you think of murdering her? Apart from anything else, how can you be sure that the house girl will not disclose your plans to your husband? Do you believe she will not leak it out? She is not a fool and so she cannot obey that cruel order from you without questioning. All you are inviting right now is police trouble which will land you with death by hanging. I must not support you, I cannot support this idea of yours at all.'

'I'm not asking you to support the idea of anything I want to do with my child. She is my child and so I have every right to do whatever I want to do to her. She's not yours. After all, you left your own children with the man you consider to be irresponsible, and I haven't said anything about it. All the support I need from you is over my marrying Idu. That is all,' I said.

'I will not do it if it means taking the life of that innocent baby!' she cried out. 'Is that how you think you can repay me for all the good I have done for you? Is that the only thing you can say after I have set you free from the bad treatment your husband was giving you? Nevertheless, you cannot stop me from carrying out my plans,' I said, standing up to go back home. But she held me back on the bed. Out of anger, I started to weep.

Deafening music was playing outside and I wondered how much money my sister would have made out of her business if I had not been there to interrupt the proceedings. 'It is all right. You can do whatever you think is right for your baby and I will not go against it. But I must warn you that the consequences will be very bad,' she said after a long silence.

'Will you help me if I run into trouble after it's all over?' I asked. She did not answer. 'Will you?' I asked again. 'Already I can see you dipping your head into the heart of trouble. I know very well that it is your own grave you are digging by taking this action. In any case, why do you need help from me? All I can do for you is to keep my lips sealed about what you intend to do...'

'You must help me because I have helped you repay your dowry,' I tried to force her.

She thought for a while. 'Though I think you are making a bad decision, I will help if it comes to repaying you for the good you have done for me.' 'Thank you very much,' I said, and got up on my feet to go back to Nassarawa. It was 1.22 am, and I wondered how I would be able to get back to my place from the International Hotel. I could not spend the night with my sister in the hotel. My husband might be back home before day time, and what would he think of me if he should find me absent from home?

'At this hour of the night you will not get any taxi to take you to your home, especially not to Nassarawa. What will you do, Onyemowo?' my sister asked. We kept on walking down the stairs. 'I don't really know what I will do. I think I will have to trek back home....'

'Trek back home!' interrupted my sister. 'But you can't trek back home when everywhere is so quiet!'

'What else do you want me to do, sleep here?' At the last step of the building, she paused and took a quick glance at me. She asked me to wait for her downstairs while she went back to the house to collect something. She would meet me in a moment. She left me at the foot of the steps as I wondered what she was going back to the house to collect. However, I waited.

After a short while, she came back to join me. 'I will go with you for half of the journey,' she said. I could not object to this so, with my sister beside me, I set out to go back home in the dark.

Chapter 14

The hour at which my husband and I would leave home to go to that grand party, to which all the medical doctors serving in the Murtala Mohammed Hospital had been invited, was approaching. I had to make sure my baby and Naomi were ready to go to Dr. Okafor's flat before four in the afternoon. I must give Eno the best bath she had ever been given, the bath that would send her on her way to that final world. I wanted to dress her in her best clothes as well. I did not want Naomi to do it for me. The baby needed some love before departing this world, the kind of love she had been waiting to receive from me since her birth but had never been given. Today would be different.

As I held my daughter in my arms at about fifteen minutes to four that Christmas afternoon, a sense of the love which I had never felt for her since she was born flickered in my heart. I realized that I was, for the first time, experiencing a feeling of natural love for her. She did not know that this was going to be her last day here on earth. Dr. Okon did not know that the baby he loved so dearly would, in a matter of an hour or two, be in the place of the dead. In the whole world, only myself, Naomi, and my sister knew what was going to happen to my baby. It would, however, only remain a secret if Naomi kept a silent lip over the whole thing.

'Naomi!' I called to get the attention of the girl who was busy washing plates in the kitchen. 'Madam,' she answered, coming to where I held the baby on my lap. 'Get me the baby's towel from the inner room.' She did not leave immediately but remained on that spot, gazing into my eyes. I repeated what I had asked her to do for me. Slowly, dragging her feet behind her, she left for the towel. Could it mean that she had not heard my first message clearly and was waiting to be instructed properly before she could carry out my instructions? What about her dragging feet and reluctance in going for the towel? The gaze! Why the gaze? She must be asking me through her bright eyes why I should waste my time in giving Eno a good bath when I knew she would not last long, I thought. But the remains of men are always given a good bath before burial, so why should Eno be an exception? Or maybe she was asking me in silence why I had taken that cruel decision about a baby I appeared to cherish very much. Perhaps she was debating whether to keep the secret a secret or to leak it out to Dr. Okon and ruin my life.

A few minutes later, she came back with the towel over her shoulder. As she placed it over my shoulder, I took a long look at her. She seemed to have grown a lot. 'Make sure you take your bath in ten minutes. We will not have anything else to do in the house today. I will take the two of you to enjoy yourselves with the children of Dr. Okafor in his flat. I'm sure there will be a little party for you there to mark Christmas. And remember my instructions,' I told her, with a warm smile from the side of my mouth. My glance held a warning.

'But... but...' She wanted to say something but soon stopped before she could articulate the words. This frightened me. Was she going to change her mind about everything? Had she already told my husband about it, and as a result, was he now preparing to stop me? And was Naomi going to tell me? I just could not tell.

'You wanted to say something to me, Naomi. What is it that you wanted to say?' I asked nervously. 'Yes, Madam,' she said, with a nod of her head. 'Then go on.' 'It is about my shoes, Madam. They don't fit my feet properly.' 'Have you not got two different pairs? If one of the pairs does not fit you, won't the other pair do?' 'I haven't got two pairs, Ma,' she said. Then I remembered that, though I had bought two pairs of shoes for her, I had not shown her the second pair. It was still in my bag inside my room. How silly of me to forget. And she had now reminded me of it. It was also very stupid of me not to try the first pair on her feet before deciding to buy the second pair.

'They are in the black bag in my room,' I told her, and she ran out, grinning. A car blasted its horn outside, which made me turn my head sharply. It was a little car belonging to Dr. Okon. He had just come back from the dry-cleaners with his jacket for today's party. I heard the car door slam, and I knew he was going to hurry me up over my preparations for the party. He had never once been satisfied with the time I took in getting my clothes on when going out with him. What he hated was lipstick on my lips, so he had never allowed me to coat my lips. In the dry weather, he had often examined every line on my lips closely to make sure that I was not cheating him.

He hurried past with the jacket across his shoulders and went into the parlor. At the door, he glanced at me, then went in. From his expression, I knew that when he came out next, he would complain bitterly over my delay. I must not do anything to hamper the success of my plan. So I doubled the pace which I was taking in preparing my baby for the long journey to the world of the dead.

'I think I must first of all take the children round to Dr. Okafor's before we leave for the party.' 'Well, do whatever is convenient to you. All I'm saying is that you must not delay things. Be ready by ten past four, all right?' I went back to my bedroom to fetch the little bag containing my money. I could not go without it. It was a part of my life. The flat to which I was taking Eno and Naomi that afternoon was just a stone's throw from ours. We could manage the distance on foot. There was nothing Eno loved more than her little perambulator. Though she was now growing bigger and bigger, she still used it. She was nearly sitting up now. With Naomi pushing the pram and leading the way, I accompanied them to Dr. Okafor's flat. As we approached the house, the deafening noise of children caught our ears. The house was already filled with the innocent ones who had come to enjoy themselves.

Naomi looked down at her new dress, glanced at me, and smiled. In a matter of minutes, I was once again back in our house. This time I had nothing much to do in the house which might consume the time left before the grand party. All that needed to be done now was to take a final look in my mirror. I could not leave the house without this final check-up. Dr. Okon was already in the car, in his best suit, ready to 'take off' for the party. After a moment, I came out. As it was getting on towards four-thirty, he put the car into gear immediately, and off we went for the party.

The room where the party was taking place was almost full when we arrived. The Minister of Health, who was chairman of the occasion, was already on his feet addressing the audience which consisted of the medical doctors and their wives, all dressed in their best. The only seats which seemed to be empty were in the middle of the room. This meant that we had to squeeze right past everybody. I felt every eye was looking at us, examining every step we took and taking account of our dress. If I had been alone, I would have retreated back home. But now that would have disgraced Dr. Okon. Because of this, I forced myself to follow him as he led the way to a seat facing the door through which we had entered.

As we went along, I felt as if every eye gazing at me was accusing me of murder. But I had not yet committed the murder. What if I tripped, I thought. How would I feel if that should happen to me? I would just lie still on the floor and pretend I had been taken ill so they would have to carry me to the hospital for revival. Perhaps that would be less embarrassing. When we reached our seats, the chairman paused in his speech and gave us a warning look. Was he also accusing me of murder? If I said that I heard the address from the chairman, I would be telling a white lie. My mind was never on the party. It was centered on what should be happening to my baby in the three-story building. Naomi must be preparing to take her outside the room in which the children would now be having their party with soft drinks and all sorts of sweet things. But other things might be happening there which I could not know about. Naomi might have mingled with the children and forgotten to carry out my instructions.

Directly opposite me, a couple were whispering something into each other's ears. I wondered what they could be saying. I was sure they were talking about me. And I thought each was probably telling the other, "That lady, there, is a witch. She is a strange woman. I'm going to rise on my feet and announce to everybody her mad intentions for her baby." I couldn't stand it any longer. It appeared to me as if the ghost of my baby, who was yet to die, was whispering into my ears,

"Mummy, why this, Mummy? Why should it be now? It would have been better if you had killed me at birth before I had the chance to see the brightness of the world. Why, Mummy? Why must you do this to me?" I felt drops of hot tears taking the path leading to my nose. Quickly, I rubbed them off with my white handkerchief. The vision disappeared. Was I just imagining what would happen to me very soon? I could not tell exactly what was happening. All I knew was that the voice that had just spoken to me belonged to Eno, my baby. Though she had not yet started talking, I knew she would one day do so, if only I allowed her to live.

I looked up and my eyes met those of Dr. and Mrs. Tenga. They smiled at me, and I smiled in return. I forced out a deadly smile at them. The fat lady inclined her head, and I knew what that meant. I knew that she was asking after Eno's health. In reply, I inclined mine, meaning that all was well with her, while actually she should by now be at the point of death. It was only a question of time before Mrs. Tenga discovered that all was not well with Eno.

The chairman had finished his address and had already returned to his seat. All I had gained from him was the movement of his lips. I did not hear one word out of the beautifully composed speech he made to us. Time seemed to be racing by. It was 5:30 p.m. By the time the drinks started circulating, I was hardly conscious of what was going on. The drinks flowed, and so did the food. Maybe I needed something hot that would help me to concentrate, something that would make me think less of what was happening to my daughter at that moment. I drank freely with the men who seemed capable of draining down their gullets a carton of beer each in less than thirty minutes. I drank so much that Dr. Okon and all the other doctors started to look suspiciously at me. But I felt nothing, except a slight mistiness in my eyes. I continued to drink.

Dr. Okon looked at his wrist-watch and smiled into my cloudy eyes. 'You did not leave the key to the house with Naomi, did you?' he asked. 'No,' I said. I could feel a heavy lump clogging the speech in my throat. 'It is here with me, in my bag.' 'I see. But don't you think you ought to take it back to her, or at least go and collect them by six? I would not like them to stay outside after dark. Eno could easily catch an evening cold, and I don't want her to do that. Do you hear what I'm saying?' he said. 'Yes, of course. I will go by six,' I said. Soft drinks flowed. Hot drinks flowed. Food, a surplus.

It was not time for the free movement of the body to disco music. The disco man had all this time been perching by the heavy musical instruments in a corner of the spacious room. He called on the chairman and the chairlady of the occasion to step forward and open the floor to other dancing feet. This received loud applause from the audience. As the four heavy stereo speakers began to vibrate, the two most important personalities stepped forward and began to make slow movements of their bodies as they danced. The duration of the music was very short. When it stopped, the two people went back to their respective seats. Another round of clapping echoed in the room.

The second phase of the music started up and brought a good half of the doctors and their wives, and even lady doctors, on to their feet. My husband and I got up. With hands on each other's shoulders, we began to dance to the music. Six o'clock. Still the drink flowed. We went back to our seats. My husband looked at me and asked if I could, please, go and fetch the baby home. I agreed reluctantly with him, left my seat and moved to the door. I felt sure that by this time the deed must have been perfectly carried out. But on getting to the door, which was almost covered by plants and flowers, a new thought began to cloud my mind. If my instructions to Naomi had really been carried out, wouldn't we have known about it long ago? The house was not that far from where we were now attending this grand party. A small insect flew from nowhere into my left eye. In an effort to take it out, tears flowed down my nose, and my eyes became red in color. As I reappeared from the flower-covered door, I looked across the road to Dr. Okafor's flat. There, on the ground floor of the building, I caught a glimpse of a crowd of fast-moving young boys and young girls. Gradually a knot of adults began to gather. Then I saw somebody running towards the house where I was now standing in perplexity. Yes, I knew what had happened. My daughter must have taken her last breath. But how could I be sure that it wasn't Naomi herself who had fallen? Obviously either she or the baby must have fallen, and it was essential for us all to rush over to see what had happened. I hurried back to the party, where the people were still having a good time, to tell Dr. Okon that something had happened to one of the children in Dr. Okafor's flat. He was the doctor for the entire family, and his help must be very badly needed there. I decided to alert his attention to what had happened, not because I loved my daughter so much that I did not want her to die, but to cover my guilt, if there was any to be apportioned. I had begun to love my daughter, but she must die for a cause. As I whispered into his ears, I tried as hard as I could to control my voice in such a way that I sounded nervous; I was pleased with my performance. Dr. Okon replaced the glass of beer he was holding in his hand on the table, got hurriedly to his feet, and took the lead as we went towards the door. I could see drops of sweat forming on his forehead. 'Did you say Dr. Okafor's flat?' he asked nervously. I nodded my head.

Dr. Okafor was still overseas on a special course. Only his wife and the children were at home. Why was Dr. Okon so worried about this news, I wondered. Had he all along suspected that something like this might come up one day? He began to run as he neared the main road. In all the time I had spent with him, I had never seen him so agitated. He ran as if he weighed nothing in spite of his bulk. I ran too, but could not catch up with him. Just before we got to the main road, we met one of the older girls who was running to tell us what had happened. She confirmed the death of my little daughter. She stammered out that it was a horrible sight. Even I did not need to be told by her how horrible the sight might be. The most stupid person on earth would not need to be told what would happen to anyone falling from a three-story building.

Where the baby must have fallen, I could see the little children gathered, crying and screaming in fear. I saw Naomi. She was crying bitterly, with her hands over her head. Why was she crying? Why was she weeping? I could not think why she should do so. Should she be weeping over what she purposely had done to the little baby? It was a splendid death!

Dr. Okon was still running as fast as he could. He crossed over the first lane of the busy road. Suddenly an enormous, heavy tanker appeared. Dr. Okon obviously thought he could cross over the road in front of it safely. It seemed that he thought he could not wait for the long vehicle to pass before continuing his dash to the opposite side of the road. He miscalculated, however. Roaring along at full speed, the 'elephant of the road' continued on its way and crushed him to the belly of the hungry road. It screamed to a halt at a distance of about twenty yards away. Oh! The sight! It was horrible.

When I saw what had happened, I knew that my dreams had really come true. The father and the daughter who had both been obstacles to my freedom were now gone. But if this was so, why did I remain standing there on my shivering feet, waiting for another chain of bondage to go round my wrist? I had to run away. But where? My sister, I thought. With the hot sweat pouring down my face, I waved down an oncoming taxi cab and boarded it for the International Hotel.

Chapter 15

The first hurdle had just been cleared and left behind, but the greater part of the problem was still ahead of me. Nevertheless, with my senior sister beside me at the International Hotel, I felt protected. From there, I would be able to make a proper contact with Idu, or at least get more information about his arrival in the country. Even if I could not go down to the airport in person, I knew my sister would go for me. Nobody would think that I had had anything to do with my daughter's death. What about any conversation Naomi might now be having with the police? It was a strange story, and if she were to tell it to the men in uniform, a cold cell in a stinking gaol would surely be my home for the rest of my days on earth. So, for the meantime, while everything was still confused, I had to remain with my sister in the hotel. It never entered my head that I perhaps ought to have stayed at Dr. Okafor's flat for a little while to see what Naomi said and to play the grieving wife and mother. 'Idu, Idu,' that was all I thought about. Yet, apart from my own people, who knew the cord that held me tight to Dr. Okon, who else did? What if I saw Dr. and Mrs. Tenga? Wouldn't it be better if I were to go to court to get everything legally ironed out? All there had been between me and Dr. Okon for the whole time I had spent with him had been only friendship; that would be what I would say to the court. And now that beautiful death had taken him away from his enjoyment of the world, why should I fear to walk with my head held high?

I did have a little pang of conscience about my daughter as I took shelter in my sister's room, but my mind was too full of my triumph to dwell on what the consequences might be. My sister's expression worried me when I ran into her room panting. Had she changed her mind about the promise of support she had already given me? 'They are both dead!' I told her breathlessly.

'Do you mean you have succeeded in killing your one and only baby, your daughter?' she asked. I did not answer. She looked accusingly at me. 'What have you done, Onyemowo? Tell me what you have done!' 'They are both dead,' I repeated. That was all I could bring myself to tell her.

She dragged me right into her room, closed the door, and asked me to tell her everything that had happened. I told her how my baby had been smashed to death and how her father was killed by the fast-moving tanker and, finally, how I had fled from the spot of the accident. She shook her head slowly and wonderingly at the news. Christmas was forgotten. I began to feel guilt and shame but, in a few days' time, Idu would be welcomed back to Kano International Airport by all the pretty hostesses who worked there.

Ever since the day I told my sister her dowry had been paid, she had been feeling a sense of total freedom. She would no longer have to keep her work in that room among those fat women. She would no longer have to go out with the fear of being spotted and embarrassed by those who knew her from her husband's home. By this time, many people had discovered that she was no longer with her husband and that she had paid back the dowry.

It was Sunday afternoon. In the town, there was due to be an Idoma Community development meeting later in the day. My sister had told me that she would be attending the meeting. She decided that, before she went, she would cook something nice for both of us to eat. The soup was still on the fire, and she was stirring it while I helped her by peeling the yam. As I was busy with the knife, I felt that I needed to talk to her about contacting Idu when he arrived, which would be the next day.

'Won't you be late for the meeting?' I asked, not wanting to dive straight into the matter. 'I will be late if we don't hurry up,' she agreed as she continued to stir the sweet-smelling melon soup. 'Get the yam peeled as soon as you can and set it on the fire. I think the soup is ready.' 'I want to talk to you.' 'Yes?'

'Idu is coming back tomorrow. I won't be able to meet him at the airport because of the fear of being recognized by the people who know me...'

'Onyemowo, get yourself together. The deed is done. I'm sure the marriage wasn't legal, so nobody has the right to demand the bride-price back. The money the man gave to our parents, as I see it, was just a gift to show that he felt love for you and nothing more. For this reason, you will just have to forget about the past, face the present, and then look forward to the future. Walk in the streets like the free girl you already are. As for Idu, you could go to the airport tomorrow and meet him. But you must realize that he is no longer intending to marry you if he is really coming back home with a white girl. She will never be prepared to share him with you. My advice to you is to forget about the marriage and start looking for another man as I will soon do. I suppose that depends on whether you are ready to marry another man,' she said thoughtfully, still stirring the soup with a big spoon.

The advice she gave me appeared unkind and I felt unable to follow it, so I told her that I could never allow the white girl to take possession of Idu without doing anything about it. 'Well, make sure you don't do anything that will make things worse for yourself. If you meet him and get a chance to explain everything that happened just before he left home and also everything that happened during his absence, and he still does not want to have you back, then you must forget about him. Try to make him realize that it wasn't for your own good that you went to live with Dr. Okon. In any case, if he comes back with the white girl, I very much doubt that he will change his mind and take you back,' she said firmly.

'He must change his mind!' I burst out, dropping the knife in my hand onto the floor. 'And if he does not, what will you do then?' 'Well...' I hadn't really thought that far ahead. 'Right now, I would like you to help me check his arrival time at the airport tomorrow morning. Would you go out and wait there? I'm sorry I don't know the exact hour of the morning he will be at the airport. I know it is a very big job I'm asking you to do for me. I am quite aware of the inconvenience involved in waiting indefinitely for someone you have never met before...'

She opened her mouth to say something but thought better of it and stopped with her mouth still slightly open. I could guess what she had been going to say. She had been going to object to going to the airport the next morning. But she had changed her mind at the last minute, realizing all the good I had done for her. Instead, she asked if it would not be better and wiser to try to get the information from the meeting she was going to that afternoon. There would be many men and women of Idu's tribe there who would be able to furnish her with news about his homecoming.

'That is a good idea. See what you can find out from them. But if you fail to find anything out, please help me by going to the airport tomorrow,' I said. But from her expression I knew that she did not like the idea of going to the airport to meet Idu the next morning.

Chapter 16

Towards seven in the evening of that Sunday, there was a terrible moment for me. It was already getting dark. As I lay on the bed, behind the curtain that separated my sister's bed from the rest of the room, I started to imagine what I might do the moment I saw the white girl coming home from the airport with Idu. I would bite off her nose and turn her into a housefly, I thought. Idu was mine and no one else's. 'Yes, he was mine,' I said aloud. I had already sacrificed my only daughter for him, I repeated to myself. The woman waiting at the door for her own luck to show up must have heard me saying this but could not make any sense of it. She must have thought that I was going out of my senses. I was tempted to try to make her realize that I was still in my normal senses, but when I touched the floor with my feet in an attempt to convince her, my heart failed me. All I could do was lie there in silence.

As I lay there daydreaming, my sister rushed into the room unexpectedly, breathing heavily. I was really scared by her rushing in like that. I immediately assumed that she had overheard people talking about my murdering my baby and how it had led to the death of Dr. Okon, and that she had run back home to alert me to the danger of showing my face in the street. The baby must be lying in a cold grave with heavy stones resting on her breast, I thought. I rose quickly to my feet, trembling all over in fear.

'What is happening? What is going on outside?' I asked. 'There's been a car accident... Idu and the white girl have had an accident and both of them have been killed. Their bodies have been taken to the hospital...' she stammered out the bad news. 'Accident! Which... which hospital was he taken to?' I only wanted to know about Idu—the girl meant nothing to me. 'City Hospital,' she answered. 'But they were not supposed to be coming today.' 'All I know is that the bodies have been taken to the hospital,' she maintained.

There was no time to waste. I could not even stop to wonder whether I might get into worse trouble by going. I grabbed the blouse that I had thrown on the floor and ran out of that lonely room towards the hospital to see if my sister was right and if Idu was really lying in the mortuary.

I tore out into the road and was lucky enough to find a taxi almost immediately. At the hospital, I flung some money at the driver and raced up the steps. I was directed to the mortuary and pushed my way through a crowd that had collected by the door. Sobbing, I asked the attendant if I could see my love. He pulled back a sheet that covered a still form... there was my beloved, his lifeless face unmarked and as handsome as I remembered it. I stumbled from that room of death where all my hopes lay shattered. As I went blindly down the steps, not caring about anything else, a strong hand fell on my arm. 'Mrs. Okon? We have some questions we would like to ask you concerning the death of the baby Eno. Would you mind coming with us?'

The world went black around me...